The Genesis of Change

LIVIA J. ELLIOT

To Fernando.
It is my greatest joy to journey through life alongside you.

Contents

Before you read, please note that my **flavour** of English is Australian. I **apologise** to everyone in advance. Please don't be concerned if you **realise** something is wrong, or think I've committed an **offence**. Who knows, you may even get used to it while **travelling** through the pages.

"Oh, no!" Someone may exclaim, but rest assured, the quotes remain **double**… at least when someone speaks aloud.

However, alchemists mind-whisper, ‘*Speaking directly into someone's mind,*’ while someone's thoughts are presented without quotes: *Just thinking, in privacy. Maybe.*

Also, shall alchemy seem unreachable, you may enquire the **Alchemical Glossary** at the end.

That said, I'm **honoured** that you're interested in my work, and hope you'll enjoy it.

Livia, a writer with Aussie grammar.

This story is told from the point-of-view of millennia-old, non-human, non-gendered beings—the alchemists. Therefore, the text uses the singular they/them for these characters. Likewise, to somehow convey this non-human nature, the prose leans towards being lyrical. You may find the alchemists' descriptions somewhat odd and surreal, and their morals and goals different from humans'.

Overall, there are mentions of induced panic attacks and other extreme emotions. One storyline follows a healer, and there are mild descriptions of an array of wounds, including amputations, severe burns, and children choking. You will NOT find mentions of gender or racial violence.

Reader's discretion is advised.

The Rector

The pursuit of knowledge is an interminable quest, the most exhilarating pathway towards elusive outcomes, often yielding more questions than answers. It brings, at any point, certainty over a single and perennial fact—awareness of one's own ignorance. There is always more to learn, so much more to comprehend, so many facets to unveil, and so many new questions to unravel.

To any alchemist, the pursuit of knowledge is the most enthralling crusade upon which to embark. The only worthy quest for an endless existence.

To The Rector, the pursuit of knowledge was the very reason to be.

Amidst nowhere and nowhen, The Rector assessed the universe. Neatly classified in alchemical elements—alive, half-alive, non-alive. Easily manipulated due to possessing the four transfigurations available to alchemists—Soul, Matter, Protean, Machina. That structure was believed to be complete, round, and whole, so thoroughly known it had not changed in aeons.

The Rector chuckled at the lie. All knowledge was, by definition, incomplete and erroneous, always meant to be expanded.

Exactly as they were aiming to do.

It had taken more time than any other mind could comprehend—but The Rector, through several manipulations, had finally found two clues of something more, of something new, of something different that could redefine The Orders of alchemists. One clue was waiting precisely outside The Towers, wishing to become an alchemist. The other lived in Amberina and needed to be studied to unlock his secrets.

With the appropriate guidance, these two humans could advance alchemy and, with it, The Orders.

The Rector would ensure it happened.

"After all, I'm the spear piercing through knowledge and guiding evolution," they whispered, vanishing back into a human world.

The genesis of change was near.

Élan

5072 Concordia Era (CE)

The thunderstorms were Élan's sustenance, their joy and excitement; a perfect moment in which nothing else but their thoughts existed, colliding with the world around and about. They coiled between the currents, the shadow tendrils of their alchemical form extending, reshaping, breaking and spawning to mimic the lightning that so fed them. Élan laughed, and their mirth rippled through their soaring shadows just before they emerged from the storm wall. The remnants of clouds circled The Towers—two edifices of obsidian and starlight, connecting dimensions and embodying the bastion of The Orders.

Yet the alchemist halted airborne and glanced down, enthralled by the woman sitting outside the Tower's main entrance. Fearless, they plunged towards her, shadows spreading just in time to glide near for a better view.

She was middle-aged, with walnut skin and long black hair tied in a bun. Her knees were sinking into a puddle of mud, yet she kept her back straight, sitting on her heels. Her fingers laced atop her lap, worn by manual work and calloused like a scribe's. She wore the staples of the peasants of Strezia; peeling, worn-out boots, muddy trousers patched haphazardly, a blouse that may have once been white, and all the signs of long-term food deprivation.

Her gaze was what Élan liked the most. Emotional, consuming, fierce. Fixed on the immense double-sheeted doors of The Towers but tracing the movements of the surrounding shadows.

"You inspect me, shadow?" Her voice was half-whisper, half-growl, respectful but challenging. A blend of tones only an alchemist could concoct—except she was none. "I'll wait until those doors open. I'll become an alchemist."

Élan's laughing caw ricocheted through their shadow-made form, and in the same instant, they soul-linked her. Through that ability, the alchemist deep-dived into her present emotions and thoughts, scavenging her mind until they perceived even her unrecognised feelings.

Áurea. So filled with hatred for the Strezian nobility she now belonged to that her memories sailed on the waves of her wrath; they shaped into her father's countenance, into the loophole that forced him to become a Nova Noble, into the despair of the ivory cage of Strezia's palace. A desire raged like a maelstrom in her furious sea of emotions. Power. To craft a key to her own future, to change Strezia and perhaps the world. A thousand other cravings harassed her, but exhaustion took the forefront, fed by the painful emptiness of starvation, the mirage-inducing dryness of prolonged thirst, and the cramps of a body forced into a single position.

Élan interrupted the soul-link after that, amused. Clearly, Áurea had sat there for days, waiting and wishing—but only a single being could grant her permission to enter The Towers, and it was not Élan.

Ignoring the woman's wrathful gaze, the alchemist slithered away in their ringlets of shadow. They crossed the long distance towards the main entrance and slipped through the slivers between the Towers' doors.

Power froze them once inside.

It compressed the world, it twisted dimensions, it blended time and space. It went beyond descriptions, piling quarters of identities to shape them into the only alchemist who'd performed the four transfigurations. The one commanding The Orders. The one beyond comprehension, even for the most seasoned alchemists. The Rector.

Unsettlingly tall, transcendentally eternal, timelessly ubiquitous. The Rector hovered above the marble floor, hooded with an obsidian cloak, wings sprouting from their temples. Feathers cascaded from the golden pauldrons, the pattern of existence engraved on their breastplate. They wore a sash of fabric-like wood, faulds of silk-like prairies, legs of copper armour and wires, sparkling to machinery. One blade hovered parallel to each forearm, metal-made and unfathomable.

Immediately, Élan reshaped their hazy tendrils, twisting and contorting into a shadow-made raven body of black beak and silver eyes. They dipped their head in silence, wings spread in a bow; it was a rule, never to speak in front of The Rector unless explicitly asked to.

"What do you think of her? She has sat there for four days," The Rector's voice was as sharp as the scimitar hovering above their forearm.

Élan folded their wings, while mind-whispering into the leader's thoughts. *There is enough wrath in that woman to change the world.*

The Rector's answering smirk threatened to curb the universe with plans only their endless existence could exploit. "Harness that chaos, Élan. It will be useful to me. She'll be a good Soul Transmuter."

Their multitudinous voice slipped off the empty, opulent hallway, and its echoes spiralled around the raven-bodied alchemist. After a moment, that command moved past them and pulled at the double-sheeted doors, aligning them with the world where that human, Áurea, awaited.

Élan straightened, watching as the doors reshaped, mechanisms clicking in place, elements recombining until the doors opened quietly and swiftly. Unfazed, the raven-bodied alchemist hopped towards that entrance and watched Áurea. She was still kneeling, resilience and vengeance coating her features, hope struggling to surface.

Their gazes met for a heartbeat, and as soon as Élan curled one wing inwards, inviting, she sprang to a stand and darted inside.

There was potential in that woman, a thirst for revenge and a desire to reforge herself seldom seen in others. But as they watched her run, panting and traipsing in the mud, Elan nursed their curiosity. The Rector had subtly implied she wouldn't fail her transfiguration, but their wording... was too purposeful. Too specific.

Áurea halted past the entranceway, gaze etched on the alchemist as she whispered, "A shadow-made raven. Are you that presence from bef—?"

Her words died off when the doors hushed closed behind her, and she noticed the dark hall. Streams of light emanated from the floor, the columns coiled on themselves, and mechanisms ticked in the background, louder the longer their silence prolonged.

Élan soared, alighting onto her shoulder. Pointing a wing towards the rightmost corridor, they mind-whispered, *'Go there, tot. I'll teach you alchemy. I'll mentor you.'*

The woman stilled, fleeting panic dashing through her eyes, understanding dawning on her face—Élan's voice had echoed in her thoughts, clearer than if physically spoken.

The alchemist soul-linked her immediately, drawn by her curated and modest gestures; yet they only found a maelstrom of questions too reasonable for a human, too unreasonable for an alchemist—where, what, how, who, what if, how come, when, *why*. Enquiries swarmed her, theories distracted her, current experience contradicted past evidence... but she pursed her lips, breathing harshly as her gaze flew through the hall. Eventually, when the shock faded, she ambled carefully through the indicated path, and Élan interrupted the soul-link; they had seen enough.

"My name is Áurea," she murmured, peering at the raven with curiosity.

'Not for long,' Élan mind-whispered back, beckoning her to a mirror-filled corridor. *'After your transfiguration, you'll find a new name to better represent you. Alchemists' identities are not like humans'.'*

"Therefore, you must have a name," she stuttered, following the instructions, and crossing the sloped corridors into the lifts. "What should I call you? Mentor?"

The raven cawed, leaping into the levers and back onto

Aurea's shoulder. *'I'm Élan, one of the ten Full Transmuters; these are alchemists who transfigured both into Soul and Matter. Humans would refer to me as a Chimera-Mason.'*

Another hop and the lever bounced, gears clicking as the doors closed.

"Never heard of double alchemical types before..." She mumbled, referring to transfigurations with the human jargon, a slight frown curling her brows. "I met a Chimera once; the alchemists that rulers call for assistance during political distress... I want to become one."

'I'll train you for it,' Élan mind-whispered, curious. Few mentees arrived knowing whatever transfiguration they wanted to pursue; instead, they were scouted or prepared beforehand by the alchemists themselves.

The lift unlocked with a soft screech, gently accelerating to displace the pair through space. Curious, Élan watched the new mentee as she mauled her bottom lip, chewing it with dedication, her scowl so tight it seemed barely able to contain her thoughts.

"If you are a Chimera-Mason..." she whispered after a while, the words decanting thoughtlessly out of her. "—that means that two types are possible. In that case, I want to be both a Chimera and a Warlord."

Élan stilled, head cocking to gaze at her with one silvery eye. She hadn't the faintest idea of what she was wishing for. Had she possessed the slightest clue of what an alchemical transfiguration implied, she wouldn't even be there, least of all craving two.

For a fleeting shard of existence, Élan wondered whatever schemes they were now involved in, especially given The Rector's nuanced command—yet they promptly discarded the thought. Whatever the leader ordered was factual; it would happen, and was already happening, as per their designs. Dwelling on it was pointless.

The lift stopped abruptly, and Élan mind-whispered a long-due answer, *'One transfiguration at a time, tot. Few did it twice like me, and that combination, Chimera-Warlord, has been achieved by only two alchemists. Now—'* The doors chaffed open into the internal, spiralling gallery, and they pointed left with a wing. *'Go there.'*

Áurea ignored the request, instead stumbling forwards, shaken and gawking at The Tower's central well. Reaching the balcony's living hallway, she leaned to glance at the sky-universe far above them.

"Is that the ceiling?" She stammered, lips pursed into a dot as she frowned. Clutching the guardrail, she peered down towards the ground-blackhole, thousands of storeys below them. "There is no floor!" A scowl contorted her features towards the tip of her button-like nose—and she gasped, watching the unending staircases branching from the spiralling balcony. "Those staircases… are the alchemists walking on the ceilings and floors?"

Élan sighed, having long forgotten the shock of witnessing the entrails of The Towers. The structure anchored into the human reality via two edifices on an island, traversing this world side-to-side and ultimately beyond the confines of physical laws. Young alchemists barely comprehended it, so a human wouldn't even fathom how it worked. Explaining would be just a waste of time.

'I'll take you to your chambers.' The raven pinched her chin, hoping to refocus her. *'Sleep. Wash yourself, tot. Your lessons have already started.'*

Still shocked, Áurea stepped away from the guardrail and followed the alchemist's instructions while muttering questions Élan didn't bother answering.

Áurea's agape mouth disclosed her renewed shock—but as most Strezian Nobles, she deftly swallowed her questions, schooling her face. Perched on her shoulder, Élan cocked their head, a silver eye watching her physical body. She had changed into the provided clean black trousers, tucked white blouse and leather boots fastened up to the calves, having bunned her hair.

"How is this possible? How were The Towers built?" The human whispered, studying the training room.

It had walls of melted marble and metal. The ceiling opened

to a galaxy's edge, and the glassy floor was built above a waterfall's descent.

'By blending elements into the dimensions, and forcing time out of the structure,' Élan stated, waving her off with a wing to prevent an interruption. *'You won't understand the how now. Perhaps in a few thousand years. Now focus there...'* They beckoned at the fireballs and airballs dancing around them. *'The first of the three alchemical elements, half-alive. Fire, water, air, plants and spores, thunder, and smoke, among others, are created, destroyed, and manipulated by a Protean Reshaper's will. As with any element, such coercion is only possible after acquiring an intrinsic understanding of the element itself. Therefore—'*

The human's lids twitched erratically. "Protean Reshapers. We know them as Warlords. The legends speak of their power." She paused, thoughtful, and rubbed her shivering arms. "If these are half-alive... there must be alive and dead elements."

'Clever, tot,' Élan cawed, spreading the wings; her questions moved in the right direction—yet they paused, mind-stating, *'Your frown is not thoughtful.'*

Áurea's cheeks puffed in embarrassment, and she averted her gaze. "I'm forty years old. Yet you... keep calling me tot."

Élan cackled, amused. Evidently, for all her carefulness and curated expressions, this simple sobriquet had exasperated her.

Delighted at the furrowing sprout, they mind-whispered, *'Your handful of decades is but ephemeral compared to the boundless, frameless existence of an alchemist, never representative of any yet all eras in equal parts.'* Lingering, they fluttered the wings to forbid yet another interruption, and soared to fly away. *'Follow! I'll introduce you to the other elements!'*

Áurea ran behind them, exuding questions and stumbling through the elements. She raised an arm as the raven approached a perceivable collision—but the wall slid open to let them cross into the next room. Granite tables occupied the area, covered with fragments of metal, wood, stone, and gemstones, alongside gears, levers, slithering wires, and objects Élan couldn't define but were common to them.

Another alchemist stood among the tables. They had wings of pole arms, a metallic arm protruded from between their shoulder blades, and their ink-made garments flickered as they assembled a contraption with incredible speed. They paused, greeting the newcomers with a nod.

'*Áurea, meet Hark,*' Élan introduced the metal-winged alchemist, returning the cordial bow. '*Hark is a Machina Reshaper, who—*'

"I recognise you!" Hark chuckled, gears clicking with the motion. "The woman sitting outside! I thought you had potential. We haven't had a human apprentice... in quite a while." Their voice chafed like metal, a gentle smile curling their oil-coated bronze-made mouth. "Are you mentoring her, Élan?"

The Full Transmuter assented, mind-whispering to both, '*As I was about to explain...*' They gestured with a wing to the parts scattered around. '*—those elements are—*'

"Oh, let *me* explain!" Hark interrupted again, catching Áurea's bewildered gaze before indicating a pile of dust with a seven-fingered hand. "I present to you: non-alive elements. Look!" They murmured unintelligible words, and the dust melted into liquid mercury. "Non-alive elements are those whose chemical composition can be altered by a Matter Transmuter's will; Masons, as humans call them. However, Machina Reshapers like me can combine existing half-alive and non-alive elements by will and knowledge." Commands sneaked from their mechanical mouth, and the mercury blended with the surrounding air, reshaping into a set of mechanisms. "See what I did? The elements are intrinsic to me; therefore, I *will* them to change."

The human gawked, stuttering, "You *will* them? Because of... your understanding?" Áurea's mouth trembled with other restrained questions, muttering a few hows and whys. She scratched her chin, frowned at the objects, and gestured nonsensically before returning to her mentor. "You said *existing* elements."

Hark chuckled in a shrieking rumble, mind-whispering only to the raven-alchemist. '*She thinks! She sparks! I can see why The Rector let her in. Would you take her to the Empty Room?*'

'*Soon,*' Élan replied, still taming their curiosity surrounding The Rector's command. Then, they fixated on the mentee, openly mind-whispering, *'You have seen two elements by now, and three alchemical transfigurations. Matter Transmuters can create, combine, and convert non-alive elements with their will and knowledge; likewise, Protean Reshapers have a similar connection to half-alive elements.'* They lingered, letting the words sink in before adding, *'However, Machina Reshapers are the only single-transfiguration connected to two types of elements, half-alive and non-alive; thus, they cannot create, just combine.'*

Within the timeless Towers, the explanation continued.

Somewhere, Áurea frowned.

Somewhen, she asked her questions.

Somehow, Hark answered and Élan taught, but not yet.

Simultaneously, Élan opened their shadow-feathered wings and surged. Their will reached Áurea's with a purposeful, irrefutable command—to soar into The Towers' dimensions alongside the mentor. Thus, the alchemist flew into the galaxy-ceiling, past the barriers of that room. Áurea didn't resist but followed closely, sprinting without realising she was climbing through the air, her hand stretched to reach for the alchemist's shadowy tendrils. The pair left Hark behind, travelling through corridors and rooms until The Towers delivered them into the Empty Room. A nothingness visually devoid of anything, sunk in darkness but full of intangible alive elements —as terrifying and distressing as only emotions and thoughts can be.

Áurea gawked at the surrounding pure blackness, but Élan willed a cluster of misery and distress, and slung it at her. The emotion hit the mentee, and she scowled, enveloped by a barrage of foreign depression—and the alchemist watched as her sadness decanted into the pitch-black pools of a death wish. When tears trailed through her cheeks, Élan summoned an opposing emotion, and flung it at her. Áurea's sorrow evanesced immediately, and she chuckled with the unmarred hope of those who haven't lived enough.

'Alive elements,' the raven introduced, melting into pure shadows. *'These are mental states like emotions, including thought patterns and social constructs, both conscious and unconscious. This is the element only Soul Transmuters can retrieve, read, reshape, and*

ravage with their will, as enabled by their knowledge. No other trans-figuration can work with alive elements.'

Their tendrils coiled around the woman, who stood amidst that blackness. Her thought patterns flared from her as well, one over the other, contradicting like her questions, incessant like her doubts, shouted so strongly they rendered her speechless—but she detached from them, letting calmness overrule every other emotion. Élan marvelled at Áurea's unconsciously practised composure, so trained and refined because a schooled countenance was a matter of life or death among Strezia's nobility.

'To transfigure into a Soul Transmuter, a Chimera as humans call us, you must understand alive elements,' Élan explained, shadows coiling around her. *'Alchemists are shaped by the elements they*

control; therefore, you can only transfigure the moment you master a frameless, reasoned comprehension of alive elements.'

"Now I see why Soul Transmuters are political advisors. These alive elements must give them an understanding of someone's mind, and of society, that is otherwise unattainable." She smirked, eyes closed, her voice trembling softly under the weight of all the emotions in the Empty Room. "Teach me about alive elements. Guide me to become a Soul Transmuter. Please."

Élan's shadows rippled to mimic the audible pattern of never-spoken words. 'The process is dire. We tap into the limits of existence and the shapelessness of past and present. During that process, while tending towards comprehension, you will lose your human identity to reform your self. The more you learn, the more Áurea will vanish until you are ready to transfigure.'

Enabled by The Towers, past the conglomeration of realities that weren't for an alchemist but were for a human, Élan existed, unrestricted and timeless. In that state, they explained the same process to a tripartite Áurea that had been, was, and would be—different words, more or less nuance, but always the same concept.

"I will learn," those Áureas promised, over and over. Then, now, and long after.

CARBONA
FOREST OF CORTEZAS
ACERO GULF
HILLS OF JADE
N
AMBERINA

Verve

5072 CE

The storm raged in the night, muting the stars and sucking in the moonlight; a perfect, fleeting moment where Verve coerced the lightning, gliding between the rampaging currents. The alchemist spread from the barrage of electricity, blending with the verdigrised clouds and coiling into tendrils of smoke. They swirled, playful, sucking air to feed their alchemical body until they broke the storm wall by striking lightning into The Towers. It highlighted the ground below, where a human woman, so full of potential, sprinted across the mud and into the open doors.

Suspended airborne, the alchemist discharged again, briefly soul-linking her to glance at her deepest thoughts; through that connection, they saw Élan's raven-shaped body awaiting inside the central hall, and a volley of revenge and hope swirling within her. The situation intrigued them, yet Verve interrupted the soul-link—they would later enquire about that human; her thought patterns were certainly unusual.

With the matter settled, the alchemist altered the air, igniting currents that delivered them exactly above the guardrail of the nearest balcony. From there, their smoke melted to slither across the obsidian-made floor, slipping through the slivers of the single-sheeted door.

Power froze them once inside.

It twisted realities, it comprehended existence, it unlocked realms of knowledge. It was formed by quarters of identities assembled into the only alchemist who had achieved all four transfigurations. The commander of The Orders. The Rector.

They awaited farther down the corridor, the sparkling machinery of their copper-wired boots flickering over the floor. The feathers cascading from their golden pauldrons shuffled with the remnants of Verve's breeze, and the golden wings sprouting from their temples fluttered as The Rector beckoned the newcomer to approach.

Verve's smoke reshaped into a neat ball and rolled through the hallway to unfold into a foggy, soot-made shape at their leader's feet. An impervious silence mingled between both alchemists until Verve cut the smoke with a grin and curled into a clumsy bow. The Rector tittered—*tittered*—and the motion rattled their crowning wings, a faint smile curling their lips.

"Effusive as always, Verve. Regardless, I saw you assessing that woman. What interested you?" Their voice was the perfect concoction of an ageless existence.

'The untamed chaos within her is unparalleled. She ripples with all elements...' Verve mind-whispered directly into The Rector's thoughts while shivering with excitement. *'If any alchemist can mentor that, it's Élan. I'll question them later!'*

"Hence, not you. Why?" The Rector cocked the head, their smile melting into curiosity.

Verve stretched, smoke splotching in sections, perturbed by the corridor's faint breeze.

'Her potential is enthralling. Her immaturity is not.' They paused, spinning and stretching the sooty smoke as if to look up. *'Do you have someone for me, Rector? It's been a few centuries already...'* Their questioning was irreverent and rule-defying, but having an immaculate trail of expeditious, successful missions had its advantages.

Unfazed, The Rector looked down at Verve's amorphous smoke. "I have something else for you. A mission."

They pointed down, and the hovering scimitar lowered to Verve's height. A reflection appeared on the blade, blurred by the distance but slowly focusing to reveal a stubbled middle-aged man with black hair and pale green eyes. The image moved as he grimaced, wriggling his hawked nose and failing to push away the strands of hair clearly tickling him.

"Go to Amberina and find Iúrdan," The Rector commanded, glancing down as the figure in the blade continued to move. "Study him; he is important to me."

Verve dismantled into tendrils, stretching and coiling to further inspect the figure. *'What do I need to study?'*

"The unexplainable." The echoes of The Rector's voice slithered through the scimitar, smudging the image.

A single question rattled Verve's mind: what could be unexplainable to the alchemist who had mastered every ounce of known knowledge by achieving all transfigurations?

'Why is he important?' Verve mind-whispered as boldly as no one else would dare.

The Rector tilted their head. "He is a key."

Verve bent, curiosity hanging around unshared. Whatever that key unlocked was relevant enough to send one of the two Chimera-Warlords on a mission presented as a mere observation—and The Rector was anything but haphazard in their decision making.

An expectant, intrigued silence ensued, creeping around both alchemists like a predator waiting to lurch. After an iota of time, before The Towers rattled under the quietude's weight, the leading alchemist smirked, mischievous—and their second-in-command reciprocated, coiling their smoke-body into tendrils recharged with lightning.

"You are after knowledge," Verve stated, willing the sound waves to spread from their smoke to embody a modulated yet flat voice. "*What* knowledge?"

"Ground-breaking knowledge," the leader stated, beckoning the scimitar to raise with a single gesture. "Study him, Verve. *Thoroughly.*"

The Rector vanished, but their voice subsisted after their departure, hissing through the empty corridor and leaving Verve with an order that could not be refused—and neither did they want to. Ultimately, their taunting impertinence was nothing more than an echo of their playful, perennially elated nature.

For the briefest span, Verve wondered whatever had The Rector foreseen in Élan's new mentee, or why this petty human was worth investigating. The Rector's choice of words had been... too purposefully intriguing, too shaped like a bait. Verve knew that, in due time, they would solve that puzzle of a mission.

If The Rector was after knowledge, Verve would oblige.

Thus, with renewed curiosity about the mission, the alchemist soared through the corridors towards the Library. Gathering information before acting was essential to any research.

The energy within the network of alchemical portals propelled Verve across the centre of the world and into Amberina's continent. They materialised far to the south and willed the air currents to soar above the clouds. Whirling between warmth and chillness, Verve reshaped into a pale, silver smoke and altered the wind's direction to speed northwards.

Amberina was a rickety peninsula shaped like a grabbing hand, with its opulent castle situated almost in the centre. Built with a coal-hued stone, the six-towered stronghold cut grimly across the green hills, reflecting with perfect accuracy on the crystalline water of the surrounding lake. The alchemist circled over the manicured, artfully styled gardens—but then willed the clouds to recharge. Their colour darkened and azure lights wriggled among them as Verve soared again, speeding further northwards into the Acero Gulf.

Once there, they overflew the port city of Carbona. It was beautifully planned and well-kept, with carefully planted trees and blossoming bushes decorating the large, open roads. Artificial canals spread through the area, draining water from the Gulf to feed the different suburbs; marble bridges connected each segment, always wide enough for horse-pulled carts to move around.

The areas fringing the Gulf were boisterous, rattling with the shouting of ravenous merchants, over-excited tourists, and locals grunting and groaning at the myriad of inconveniences slowing their daily life. Yet from their vantage point in the clouds, Verve willed the wind again, aiming further west and away from the shore. Slowly, the noise receded alongside with the masses of humans, the roads thinned, and the canals ended in fancy fountains.

It was noon when Verve reached their destination, lowering their altitude to take in the fringes of Carbona. Everything was simpler in this town, smaller, and more silent than near the shore. The central plaza was barely a dot on the map, the merchants' stalls lacked the vibrant colours, and the houses—albeit marble-made—were flatter, larger, and harbouring gardens, stables, or other appendages.

Trailing the roads, Verve flew towards Iúrdan's house. The road leading there was populated, with pedestrians moving around at the sluggish, depressing pace surrounding any clinic. The house itself reeked of the alive elements—thought patterns, emotions, and mental states—so often seen in patients, acting like a beacon to the alchemist. When they halted airborne, their perception flooded with the colours, scents, and shapes of a hundred emotions.

Fear oozed like poisonous gas, moaning and wailing with all the varied sources that could cause it. Anxiety and distress spread like shaky snakes, coiling skywards or lurching into any of the unfortunate passers-by. Disgust slashed everything else, empowered by the distress of humans attempting to imagine the source of the metallic noises and muted voices.

Halting in the clouds with an implicit command, the alchemist plunged like a strand of silverish smoke, and alighted onto the slanted rooftop of their target's house. Rolling over the edge, they slipped through the open main door and hid in a corner.

The waiting room was large, lined with the same white marble that characterised Amberina, and reflecting the noon's silvery light that blasted through the open doors and windows. Wooden, cushioned chairs lined every wall, all occupied by an assortment of humans—from tourists to locals, from rags to riches, all sat down with the same expectant gloom coating their varied features. A handful remained standing, sometimes posing a hand on another's shoulder, while a toddler sprawled on the floor, playing with her toys and laughing with unrestrained mirth. A natural breeze whizzed by, both cold and warm, and clogged with the juxtaposed odours of disease, nervous sweating, and medicinal herbs.

Finding no use for those patients, Verve slipped to another corner, intent on finding the healer—but a door creaked open, disrupting their plans. The waiting crowd perked and brightened, the hope of being called next vanishing their bodily distress.

Iúrdan emerged from that open door, black-greying hair collected into a small bun, a white apron tied over his well-worn trousers and tunic. His thin lips curled into a dutiful smile as he walked slowly, lending his elbow to the elderly woman beside him.

From that corner of the ceiling, Verve assessed the man, not bothering to soul-link him. To the alchemist, such ability only enhanced their natural perception, adding a level of detail seldom needed—especially when Iúrdan oozed the dauntless inner peace universally achieved by every long-standing healer. It implied a complete, logical acceptance of one's lack of control, matured from the understanding of the myriad of intersecting and opposing agencies exerted by millions of humans. It was the peace taught by his profession, derived from too many cold and calculated decisions, and developed after losing too many and caring too much.

Restraining any prejudice towards the ordinary human, Verve watched as Iúrdan guided the elder towards an anxious youngster. They exchanged a few pleasantries, and the healer repeated his advice with a cadence that verged on caring. After a repetitious exchange of farewells, the man turned to the waiting room and noticed a young woman dressed in an expensive draped dress.

"Lady Mara, I have your medicine," he stated, halting her interruption. "Please, wait here."

He dashed out towards another door, and Verve transmuted into the breeze itself to trail behind. Iúrdan swerved into an internal corridor, sandals pattering over the polished floors before shirring to a stop near a closed glass door. It blurred the inside of a greenhouse, yet the healer ignored it, instead turning to fiddle with an open cupboard of black-dyed wood. After a few moments of sorting through dozens of flasks and pouches, Iúrdan produced one and rushed back to the room.

Yet as the alchemist followed, invisible to anyone, a realisation dawned on them—through that entire ordeal, his pesky peace had continued like a flattened sound wave, so perennial and innate it dulled everything else. There had been no hurry, no eagerness, no memories surging unabridged from the human —and that realisation stunned Verve, distracting them from the shallow conversation of the healer with his patient.

Could it be that the human was so peaceful that he challenged Verve's natural perception? The one allowing them to gauge alive elements without a skill?

Curious, Verve soul-linked Iúrdan, expecting the blast of drastically redefined thoughts and feelings—but nothing changed. His thought patterns remained limited to the instructions he was whispering to Lady Mara, while experiencing a complete emotional detachment. The playing toddler laughed loudly in the waiting room, a man's chair shrieked as he shuffled in place, someone coughed roughly, and a couple whispered —yet the healer remained unperturbed and calm as he walked Lady Mara out of the waiting room and towards her waiting carriage.

Never in the last few centuries had Verve perceived such *peace*. Iúrdan embodied it, leveraging it to subsist because, to him, the certainty of living was limited to the next breath and nothing else. His mental state harboured no expectations, no hopes, no plans for anything more than the next word, the next gesture—and even that was so learned and practised that the healer acted almost thoughtlessly.

His voice surged through the soul-link, calm and focused on Lady Mara, yet the rest of the connection was uncannily *empty*.

To Verve, such peace was a nuisance. An obstacle to be disturbed in the pursuit of unexplainable knowledge.

Through millennia, and guided by alchemy, Verve had confirmed the basic principle of alive elements. Every mental state, even those sustained through decades of unbridled—and sometimes unknowing—practice, could be perturbed. Any could be shattered and splintered to release a new, sullied state; even Iúrdan's peace. The weapon was always different; sometimes simple like a sound, a memory, a word, or a gesture, yet sometimes complex like being in a specific place, or experiencing concrete sequences of events.

In particular, Iúrdan's mental state, woven with composure and courteous unconcern, was a shield against the endless projectiles shot by his profession—the daily suffering of others, the misery of loss, and the plausible impossibility of healing every patient. Thus, as a first step, Verve only needed to test the strength of that shield and find the triggers that could perturb the healer's peace in order to understand it.

Decided, Verve crept down the wall, still shaped like smoke and glamoured to invisibility. Once on the ground, they slithered through the chairs and climbed onto the decorative, minuscule table at the centre. From there, they assessed the assortment of low-risk patients in search of the perfect one to weaponise.

The whispering couple could certainly rouse emotions if something happened to any of them. Likewise, if the well-dressed son on the corner fell down, his elderly father would be scared to death. Yet neither option convinced Verve. Neither had the shattering force that appealed to bards to translate tragedies into songs, nor the shocking impression that could fuel lifetime nightmares.

Slowly, Verve turned around the table to gauge the toddler now kneeling on the ground. She was young, dressed in a tunic too clean and well-kept given her age, and with a tousled braid clustering her red hair. Her face was spattered with freckles, and her brown eyes brightened with joy as she rolled a wheeled, wooden-made horse from side to side. A freckled redhead sat near the opposite wall, her gaze never leaving her child.

From that pair, Verve judged the daughter to be the wounding weapon, and the mother the killing one.

Decided, the alchemist soul-linked the youngster, inspecting her rampant emotions. Her awe of watching the horse's wheels, and her bewilderment at the noises. The fictitious story she was imagining to fence the boredom of that waiting room, and the prairies she'd envisioned for that horse to run. She was experiencing the addictive blend of naïve inquisitiveness that could disguise any alchemy as a mere accident—yet the stage had to be set before anything could happen.

Monitoring the child's intentions through the soul-link, the alchemist willed the smallest, pin-sized bubble to emerge near the toy's wheels—and pressurised the air within. When she moved the horse, Verve released that bubble, slashing the wheel's axis. It cracked, and the rear-left wheel detached from the toy.

The girl's soul-link flared with the despair of having broken a beloved toy—but in a fraction of a heartbeat, Verve magnified the soul-link, spreading open her alive elements into crystal shards, each carved with the nuances of the thoughts and emotions they represented. Before that heartbeat ended, they found the shard creating that despair and smothered it, quelling her desire to cry. Slowly, she sat back on her heels, watching the broken toy—and Verve captured another emotion, soul-shaping it into curiosity and mischief.

The alchemist's following command was furtive and spoken directly into her mind. *'Swallow the wheel.'*

On cue, the girl picked the wheel, pushed it into her mouth, and swallowed hard. She coughed, retching—but Verve's soul-shaping forced her to swallow over and over, while mindlessly ignoring the pain searing her throat. The alchemist persisted, methodical, forcing her to ingest and lick her lips, while muting down her voice enough to disguise the accident amidst the regular noise of that waiting room. After all, she was nothing else than a tool to be used and exhausted in the alchemist's first experiment.

As the toddler choked, the other patients whispered and

talked, horses neighed outside, and Lady Mara's carriage finally rolled down the road.

Assembling a strategy meant to trigger on their command, Verve also soul-linked the mother, soul-shaping her mind. Flooding her with paralysing shock, the alchemist blocked her reasoning, forcing her wide eyes to etch on her dying daughter —but her body remained seated, too stunned to react.

"She's choking!" Someone shouted in panic, alerting the other patients. "Iúrdan! Hurry!!"

Verve's invisible smoke soared to the ceiling, and they focused on the three active soul-links—Iúrdan's, the girl's, and her mother's—as the healer rushed inside, gaze etching into the gagging child. She was scraping at her neck with increasing desperation; her face had reddened, and her eyes watered.

As methodical as the alchemist, Iúrdan acted with haste and control, unfazed by the normality of choking children. He ordered the patients to clear the room, rounded on the table, and knelt beside the girl. Moving her braid aside, he rolled her to the side and perused her mouth, precise like the scant emotions emanating from his soul-link.

A list of actions. A fleeting image of the wooden toy. The girl's waning colour. The awareness of the need to hurry, and the training to remain calm. Her sharp and pointless gasps for air. His gentleness while wrestling her scraping hands open. His concern for the mother, and his worries about the daughter. The bulk—

Mayhem exploded through the soul-link as Iúrdan's pale eyes focused on the wheel stuck in the child's throat. The jitters of shock rippled through the connection, scented with the urge to act, to heal, to save—and Verve revelled in that reaction, so common and scared it broke through the healer's inner peace. For a moment, his desperation blasted across the room, paralysing his hands—but his training rapidly overpowered that mind-clogging nuisance.

Sitting on his heels, Iúrdan turned the girl around, leaning her over his forearm and leg. His soul-link quieted again, rumbling with the steady murmuring of a mental diagnosis— and Verve observed, studying each alive element with the focus of a researcher expecting the unexplainable. Fisting his right hand, Iúrdan gave the child quick, forceful blows between the shoulder-blades, and she coughed, eyes widening with the impulse to retch again.

'Swallow,' Verve commanded, the order resonating, indisputable, in her mind.

She gasped and swallowed again and again, but the healer leaned her forwards to repeat the procedure—yet while a fragment of Verve forced her to ignore the urge to cough, another focused on the mother's soul-link, gauging her feelings.

The guilt of watching and doing nothing. The panic of losing her only child, the anguish and misery of her acknowledged powerlessness. The distress of a broken heart, the pressure on her chest caused by a pain that nobody should endure. The disbelief that it could happen to her, and a shock so profound that albeit she felt the need to rush towards her dying daughter, her body remained seated.

An elder slumped in the chair beside her, grabbing the redhead by the shoulders and shaking her—but she was unresponsive, barely blinking, jaw trembling so forcefully her teeth rattled. The alchemist was building an emotional dam on the mother, and Iúrdan would never forget the moment it released.

This isn't working. Iúrdan thought so abruptly, so strongly and explicit that the mind-words burst through his soul-link, distracting the alchemist. *I could push the object. No, it could break her throat. It won't heal, but she may survive.* His thoughts echoed again, agony and urgency underlining each word. *There may be a chance...*

The deliberate, disciplined planning enthralled Verve, and they paused the mother's soul-shaping to reassess Iúrdan; he was repositioning the child into a half kneel, with her back towards him. Bracing an arm around her abdomen, he thrust upwards, whispering soothing words. She gasped, and Verve intercepted her need to cough, again forcing her to swallow.

Someone swore and stomped out of the room. The elder raised his voice. A woman wept outside the open doors.

Judging the tension to be adequate, Verve returned to the mother's soul-link, intent on unleashing that dam and, with it, the killer blow. They soul-shaped her shock into fear of death, enhancing her guilt and letting her panic flow unbridled. She didn't move for a moment, but then her soul-link darkened and narrowed like her vision, and she howled in desperation. Jolting from the chair, she stumbled towards her child, hands extended to clutch at the healer's shoulder and pull him back. He groaned, clenching his teeth and resisting, but the woman leaned over, clawing at his bare arms until the girl fell from his arms.

He sprawled back as the mother caught the child, tucking the strands of red hair out of the blue-hued face. She moaned, cleaning the foam from her daughter's mouth, and pressing the bulk on her throat. The mother's misery was so abrasive, so staggering and devastating, that Verve severed that soul-link before letting the child's fade away—after all, dead humans produced no alive elements.

As the room dulled and the emotions blurred, Verve turned their full attention towards the healer. He struggled to a stand, grimacing yet uncaring of the bloodied streaks on his forearms. His bun was tousled, and when he peered over the shrieking woman, his shoulders slumped and the soul-link blanked into the realisation of having lost yet another patient. It was pervasive, persistent, and unpreventable; a prescription in a healer's life, an expected misfortune, a tragedy that could happen to anyone, anywhere, anywhen.

The mother wailed again, hiccuping and mumbling incoherently, but Iúrdan sighed, massaging his forehead. His soul-link was a thunderstorm of anxiety and remorse, shame and sorrow, all lashing like lightning and rattling his breathing—but as the healer turned to herd the remaining patients out into the streets, his countenance remained as collected as humanly possible.

The midnight sky was starry and silver, casting an azure hue over the world. It filtered through the glass ceiling of the healer's greenhouse—the one he'd approached that morning—adding to the heavy gloominess of his emotions. He sprawled in the lectus placed in a corner, an untouched drink clutched in his right hand, gaze lost on the plants.

Marble flowerbeds lined the walls, each busting with trees and bushes of controlled size. Large tables stretched through the centre, topped with pots with a hundred herbs, and creating ails to move through. A few shelves protruded on the opposing walls, bent under the weight of fertilisers and tools no doubt useful to the healer.

Verve rode the breeze, slithering near Iúrdan. He had remained in that lectus for almost three hours, thoughts so still the alchemist marvelled at his regained inner peace. His arms were wrapped with loose bandages, pressing the blend of herbs he had added to treat the claw marks of that desperate mother.

Iúrdan sighed at that moment, the motion releasing air but also bubbles of remorse and guilt, each vibrating with different sounds—a howl like the mother's, gagging noises like the child's, crying like someone on the waiting room, mindful breathing like Iúrdan's. The scent of blood and sweat overwhelmed the clogging odour of herbs and flowers, and Verve soul-linked him again, seeking more detail.

"Death is natural; unavoidable," Iúrdan muttered, barely moving his lips. "My actions were sufficient. Struggle is nat—"

He jerked, spilling his drink, a sudden panic slashing through his restrained peace. Still shocked, he grimaced at the half-empty drink, downed the rest, and left the glass on the nearest table. Closing his eyes, he pressed both hands into his face, muttering the same words over and over.

The alchemist followed the voice as it blended into the healer's thoughts, swirling above him and piercing the leftover fear. Iúrdan's self-control was laudable; derived from decades of practice, hardened by the externalisation of tragedy and the acceptance of death's inevitability.

Yet as unusual as it was, strenuous to achieve and onerous to apply, Iúrdan's mindset was explainable. Delimited by the alchemical rules of alive elements. Confirmed in Verve's experiment and proven by his reaction. Corroborated by the following responses, and the most thorough soul-link the alchemist had ever completed.

"Death is natural," Iúrdan whispered, slowly falling into a cadence. "Struggle is natural."

To Verve, Iúrdan's humanity was as undeniable as the mind tricks he applied to himself. Those were as unquestionable as his identity as a healer, as the memories that composed him, and the threads of the past that flared whenever he thought. Iúrdan was human and flawed, smothering his anguish because, unless he detached from feeling, his profession as a healer would deadly wound his mind.

"Death is natural and unavoidable. My actions were sufficient..." his voice slithered in that quiet night.

Except The Rector had stated the contrary.

The Rector. The leader whose plans were a convoluted labyrinth of untraceable decisions. The four-transfigured alchemist who seldom interested themselves in the ordinary. The one who existed beyond dimensions and time-frames had deemed this human to be *unexplainable*.

That command was a confounding statement meant to hide The Rector's true intentions while suggesting enough to be the most enticing enigma Verve had encountered in centuries. More than a mission, it was a game; one where the leader baited their closest one with a convoluted arrangement of demands.

Verve, the very being who fed on the exhilaration of reshaping knowledge only for the sheer excitement of learning. Verve, to whom self-improvement brought the most thrilling pleasure amidst an endless existence. Verve, who wouldn't bend nor ask for an answer, instead going to extreme lengths to develop it on their own.

Enthused by the challenge, the alchemist set to observe the human. They would not leave the riddle unsolved—especially if it led to the discovery of groundbreaking knowledge.

Élan

5072-5074 CE

Enabled by The Towers unfathomable structure, Élan weaved a network of out-of-sequence and out-of-time lessons, meant to train all Áureas on the nature and use of alive elements.

Élan delivered some lectures to past-Áurea, the newcomer who had just arrived. Others to then-Áurea, the woman eager for knowledge and awed by her mentor. More to half-human-Áurea, the mentee already experimenting with alchemy. A few were for all at once. A handful was for the Áureas that hadn't yet come.

Likewise, some lessons were theoretical, and meant to ease concepts and clarify experiences. Others were practical yet innocuous, enabled by an array of humans collected for that purpose. The last group was simply meant to destroy her identity to reshape a new one.

Within The Towers, Élan began teaching that grid of lessons.

The vast Library spread around mentor and mentee, stacks of books and rolls filling shelves that faded into the infinite ceiling. It was timeless and cross-dimensional, just like The Towers. Thus, some papyri had already been written and others would be, but the alchemists filed and read them as if they already were, irrespective of their timeline.

Élan's shadowy tendrils hurled books to half-human-Áurea, page-like wings flipping as they arched towards her. She struggled to pick the books airborne and add them to her mind-stretch—a Chimerical skill binding written words to someone's will to create a living, searchable index of content in their minds. When Élan halted their violent slinging of knowledge, they morphed into their raven-form and soared towards a table. Alighting, they assessed half-human-Áurea.

She was thinner than all other Áureas, and gold-rose locks blended with her black ones. The pale feathers protruding from her left shoulder rustled with the Library's living breeze, their shushing disrupting the quietude. She stood with arms half open and five mind-stretched books floated before her.

"Treatises by Oriana, the political advisor," half-human-Áurea frowned in concentration, whispering passages from all books. "Power balance as a cornerstone to prevent or cause war... The perceived ability to defend a population as a reinforcement of authority... A rising power as a catalyst of violence..."

Élan soul-linked her, experiencing her thoughts as she speed-read the books. They analysed her mind-stretch, assessing how she indexed the writing and searched for words by will alone. The pages flipped, coerced by her whims—but she still drowned in bewilderment, the shackles of human morality tarnishing her comprehension. Yet through the soul-link, Élan noticed that half-human-Áurea didn't have as many enquiries as past- or then-Áurea had.

'Voice your thoughts, tot. Own them,' the raven instructed, curious.

"Oriana argued that balanced power reinforces authority. This is because populations often consider that a ruler capable of withstanding inconveniences can therefore retain their power during turmoil," half-human-Áurea stated, confident. She flicked her metal-coated forefinger, and through the mind-stretch, pages flipped in a book. "When another person or state gains enough power to challenge that balance, the status quo is at risk... yet what the change implies is always uncertain. Humans cannot foresee the future, but history tells us that most changes altering the power equilibrium are violent... thus reinforcing its inherent risk."

Élan nodded, disrupting the soul-link. Within The Towers, she was also a previous version of herself, also talking to the alchemist. Therefore, the pair continued the conversation in another time, years ago for the mentee, but now for Élan. The same ideas and questions shaped into the logical pattern of training, but scattered across years for Áurea.

A matter of perception, of framing.

A consequence of her humanity and Élan's existence.

An experience enabled by The Towers.

The alchemist's shadow-feathers rustled as they glanced at her askance. *'Risk. Uncertainty. They share an underlying factor. What is that factor?'*

Past-Áurea struggled, a single book held between her hands, pages flickering between timelines. "Violence as a possibility, either offensive or defensive. For example, to force an enemy or subdue a population. But—" She stammered, haunted by questions she would never ask. "The geography matches Strezia's surroundings, but I don't recognise these countries, Élan. I know my history; they never existed. How can—?"

The raven shrugged, a wing waving back and forth to stall her pointless inquiries. *'Within The Towers, everything was, is, and would be. Time is not here. Existence is factual. If it exists, somewhen, it exists within The Towers—either recorded in the Library, charted in the Map Room, or somewhere else. But don't concern yourself with that; The Towers are unfathomable for young alchemists.'* Dropping the chastising tone, Élan pointed a hazy wing towards a book. *'You haven't answered me. What is the underlying factor?'*

The conversation continued, not then but now, seamlessly to Élan.

Half-human-Áurea spread her arms, rose-gold-black hair coiling over her feathered shoulder. "You asked me before when I hadn't understood. The future is always the underlying factor. What would or could happen *is* the risk and the cause of uncertainty. But to answer your current question, the future affects decision-making. Rulers decide based on the framed lives surrounding them, because populations voice the perceptions legitimising a leader's authority based on the perceived risk of uncertainty. After all, popular recognition *is* power, and it can be eroded."

Suddenly, both Áureas gasped. An idea illuminated her faces, and the books fell down and back through time.

'I see you pouting. Why?' Élan asked thrice, then-now-and-later. Then, when they taught her to mind-stretch; now, when together they mourned the spell she'd just broken. Later hadn't come yet.

"Politics," then-Áurea had answered long ago when pouting at a single book. "I know Soul Transmuters—Chimeras—work in politics, but I want…" she stammered, watching her human, walnut-skinned hands. "I want to learn alchemy. There is always time for politics."

'What do you think we are doing?' Élan mind-whispered, shaking their head at the startled mentee. They cawed, displeased, too firm to be didactic. *'Alchemy is around and within us. Politics are governance, from the individual level to a state-wide level… it affects and causes all alive elements, and thus concerns us.'* They hopped onto her featherless past-shoulder, one wing embracing her head, inky feathers weaving into the black hair, as they whispered, *'I'll teach you to mind-stretch. The books will explain why politics are inherent to alive elements and, thus, Soul Transmuters.'*

Through that faint touch, Élan connected to then-Áurea, letting her experience a mind-stretch. Following the alchemist's will, she lifted her arms, allowing their combined wills to weave the written words into a contained network of knowledge. Élan's shadow-feathers moved as if flipping pages, and the books obeyed, moving back and forth as willed by the mentor and their mentee.

When they landed on a specific page, Élan pinched her cheek with their beak. *'Do you comprehend? Politics. What's the underlying factor?'*

At another time, half-human-Áurea stopped pouting, the

metallic finger clicking relentlessly against her belt buckle. She was scowling at the fallen, scattered books.

"A specific emotion, which I just experienced," half-human-Áurea muttered, embarrassed as she kicked the books flattened on the ground. She'd broken the mind-stretch, and now grimaced at her mess. "An alive element. Fear. States warre because they fear the future or another's power. People fight because they fear being imposed someone else's will. I dropped the books because I feared breaking the mind-stretch and delaying my transfiguration. Fear underlies everything."

A thousand intersecting, juxtaposed conversations happened in every hall, in every waking moment, in every dream and nightmare. Élan wove all those discussions, leading Áurea to comprehend the root causes of the world as Soul Transmuters experienced it. They presented historical texts, journals, and audio recordings enabled by the devices of another era. Through them, mentor and mentee hypothesised about primal emotions, harnessing the whys and whats most Áureas questioned.

Élan taught, weaving those lessons into that network of training. Thus, half-human-Áurea evolved, while then-Áurea broke, cracked, and diminished.

Once that happened, Élan added the next type of lessons.

'Correct. Fear is a primal emotion.' Élan's thought-voice reverberated through the soul-link and into her mind. 'And your perception of it is too human,' they reproached, a wing pointing forward.

"I am human," past-Áurea rebuked, walking and glancing at the raven perched on her shoulder.

'We must rectify that,' the alchemist cawed, blending into shadows.

The Empty Room was an overwhelming void, and Élan

soared through it, alighting paces ahead. When Past-Aurea reached them, she peered through the glass floor and gasped. A brown-haired man knelt under it, famished and surrounded by infinite darkness.

"Who is he? Where is he?" The mentee asked, another myriad of questions bursting through the soul-link. She never voiced those enquires, so trained she was by Strezia's court.

'You are asking the wrong questions,' Élan admonished, willing some tendrils to creep through her legs, others pushing through the glass floor to reach the man. 'A better approximation is to ask when he is... or, more accurately, when does his mind believe to be?'

"His mind? When—?" She yelped, shuddering as she noticed the tendrils on her legs. "What are you doing!? Let me go!" Past-Áurea kicked and fought, eyes widening in distress. "Let me go!!"

Ignoring her, Élan slithered the tendrils through her spine, holding her arms to coil around her neck. Once they secured the mentee, they strengthened the soul-link and sourced variants of a single emotion from the captive man.

Fear.

Past-Áurea wrestled again, almost perceiving that amorphous, intangible mass of alive elements—but Élan remained agnostic to her distress. Extracting the first rush of fear from him, they pushed it through the soul-link and flooded past-Áurea.

She experienced the fear but didn't understand it was extrinsic to her. That confusion sparked other emotions—alive elements—cluttering her mind. The tickles of impending doom crawled through her back, and the goose-bumps of realisation blossomed on her arms. Panic chilled her as it came closer, tighter, firmer, darker.

Satisfied with what the soul-link showed them, Élan unfurled another mass of fear from the man, and force-fed it to the mentee.

That renewed terror chased her heart into an erratic gallop, twitching her cheeks. Her eyes darted across the shadows of the Empty Room and towards the inky tendrils that transferred it. The captive man saw her and wailed—and Áurea clutched her chest, fisting it, falling to her knees with mouth agape. Saliva tickled the glass amidst her silent war-cry, and their shared panic dwindled her vision.

The soul-link darkened with her twisted perception, but Élan approved of the reaction. Letting her stew in that misery, they unrolled the last mass of fear and swarmed the connection with it.

That absolute, irrevocable panic guided her towards a single conclusion. Death was coming. All around her, unstoppable and insurmountable. It was there, intangible yet truthful, eating past-Áurea's mind with the certainty that something was insidiously wrong, dangerously close, and eager to destroy her.

Élan's silver eyes flashed open amidst the shadows—the soul-link was too intense, too tight. They couldn't leave past-Áurea to experience that panic for too long, or her mind would shatter forever.

'Think, tot. Reason. Is the fear real?' Élan urged through the soul-link, tapping Áurea's hidden thoughts. 'Find what causes the fear.'

"I'll die..." She coughed, gasping for air, clutching her chest. "It's here; it'll kill me." She screamed, so akin to a man on a battlefield.

Élan sighed, tensing the tendrils around her neck and impressing their own detachment upon her mind. 'Find the cause.'

"It's not here; it's everywhere!!" She screamed again, clawing her scalp.

'Precisely!' The alchemist mind-stated, forcing their instructions past the woman's confusion. 'When does the fear come from? Think, tot!'

"All around! They'll kill me! The arrows—!" A scream, a blackout, a panting desperation wrenched from past to present.

'Are you in a war now? Is he in a war now? I'm asking when not where,' Élan intoned, didactic. 'It was logical; it is illogical! Think of the when!'

Frustrated, Élan interrupted the connection, severing the stream of fear from the man to past-Áurea. The room cleared immediately, but the terror lingered—whimpering through her lips, and sprinkling her skin with chills.

"I... thought I was dying..." She heaved, hands curling around the tendril on her neck. "You almost... killed me."

Élan chuckled, and their shadows rippled mirthlessly. *'Did I? Or was it your scrambled brain?'* Releasing her neck, the alchemist pointed an inky ringlet to the man beneath the glass floor. *'Or his? Or one of his memories?'*

For a while, there was no answer, and Élan reshaped into their raven form. Soaring, they repositioned before the woman, watching the befuddlement wane her features and curl her mouth into a grimace.

'Think, Áurea. Fear is an alive element. You must understand it to wield it, and to do so, you must live through it,' the alchemist admonished, spreading the hazy feathers to point at her. *'When was the cause of that fear?'*

"The cause?" Past-Áurea gawked and rolled a hand in distress. "It was that battlefield he fought in long ago. Somehow... something felt similar to the eve of the battle, and the similarity reanimated the long-dead fear within him."

Interested, Élan dug into the never-broken soul-link following her thoughts, conscious and unconscious, to ask the question that could spark an answer. *'What felt similar?'*

"The lack of hope," she uttered, distraught.

'That's just fear's counterpart,' Élan hissed, waving a dismissive wing. *'What else felt similar? Think! That similarity causes the fear, then and now!'*

Áurea chewed her lips, sitting on her heels and clutching her chest. Her other hand scratched her pants, eyes unfocused.

"The similarity was the uncertainty and the risk. Whether or not he would survive; what would happen if his side lost the war." She paused as a tear rolled down her puffed cheeks. "I've never experienced terror like that... it was the memory of a war, but also a war against myself. The fear happened in the past, but was real in the present."

'Indeed, so let me teach you this. Emotions are never unsourced; they always have a cause. However, as you realised, that cause may have happened long ago, instead of now. After all, emotions are alive

elements, and alive elements are atemporal,' the mentor stated into her mind, factual and dogmatic.

"Atemporal?" She asked, rubbing the saliva from her chin. "How can emotions be atemporal?"

Élan sighed, shadows splotching with the gesture. '*Because one event in your time-framed sequence of a lifetime can spark fear further as you live on. Likewise, a joyful afternoon can bring a smile years after the fact. Alive elements are not linear.*' They paused, beckoning the man below the floor, before explaining, '*He once feared the war, dying, or being enslaved. A similar uncertainty retrieved that fear, and that panic attacked you now. Why did it happen?*'

Anxiety and glumness. Alienation and rejection. Uneasiness and zeal. Agitation and bitterness. Desire, attraction, and fright. Horror and resentment. Pleasure and rapture. Glee and ecstasy. Wrath and regret. Remorse and grief. Envy, longing, and frustration. Torment and anguish.

Élan found humans suffering all those emotions—and just like before, they soul-linked all Áureas to those specimens, sinking her into maelstroms of feelings. Soon enough, those alive elements became part of her, shaping her view of the world. They shattered her ethics and thoughts, fractured her morality, and splintered her *self*.

It was all carefully planned. Timelessly consequential.

While those individual experiences became part of her, while all Áureas experienced the atemporality of emotions, Élan wove in debates to teach her the larger picture.

"Because unpredictability leads to chaos, Élan," half-human-Áurea stated, glancing at the raven on her shoulder. "Chaos becomes constant panic, which turns into a perennial emotional instability. Do it to a society, and you can topple rulers."

'Precisely. Unpredictability is the nemesis of balance... or the means to achieve it,' Élan mind-whispered, stretching a wing to point at the leftmost stack of books.

The Writing Room was noisy that day. Whispers threaded through the space, falling down from all timelines into the brushes that wrote them down. The walls and furniture were obsidian-made, and mechanical contraptions carried stacks of recently written paper while bringing more blank sheets. Purple sconces illuminated the area, alchemical arms bound stacks into books, and other gadgets ushered them back into the Library proper.

Half-human-Áurea traipsed around a small device but ignored it.

"Balance is only achieved when there is no incentive for contending people to deviate from their political strategy. It applies to rulers and peasants alike," she chuckled, tucking a rose-gold lock with a metal-coated forefinger. "That unpredictability is the enabler of chaos. It sows the fear of what could be, thus forcing people to remain as they are."

'Yet that enforced balance corrupts the status quo into something else,' Élan cawed, spreading their wings and soaring. *'Follow me! I have something to show you!'*

The alchemist flew, avoiding the alchemical contraptions and speeding because they knew half-human-Áurea sprinted behind, following. As usual, The Towers guided the pair as they ran, sliding doors open, coiling corridors, and delivering them into the Cartography Room.

A handful of Soul Transmuters occupied the area, but they ignored the newly arrived pair, instead focusing on the layered map taking the entire room. The floor was a blueprint of the world, and the ceiling's topography displayed the current destination of the time-framed humans. Other maps layered between floor and ceiling, charting a myriad of geopolitical decisions.

Élan alighted on Áurea's feathered shoulder, and pointed a wing to the map's layers. *'What do you gather from those slices hovering mid-air? Those between floor and ceiling.'*

"I assume those are different states of political order. Variations, if you will," half-human-Aurea shrugged, rustling her tousled feathered hair. "The vacuum in between is the unpredictability of the mobs, the obscurity of the public opinion, and the deception caused by war as a confounding medium." She walked, bending her left arm for Élan to perch more comfortably. "Humans comprehend none. Their emotions, ideals, and crusades confine them to a path… which may be undesirable in the larger scheme of geopolitics."

The alchemist puffed their chest, proud and eagerly pushing their thoughts towards her. *'Humans dwell in informational uncertainty. Their political realities, their avoidance of threats, their construction of appearances, and their poor management of the mob's emotions cause a number of problems,'* Élan explained, beak pointing at the different layers. *'The most important of those problems is that human rulers decide based—'*

"No. They *don't* decide; that is the problem," half-human-Áurea interrupted, enthusiasm speeding her words. "Humans *don't* decide because they fear everything you listed. Thus, their political constructs decay while enforced in place, because leaders dread the violent retribution or the loss of power any change could bring."

Élan's feathers morphed into shadows, spreading upwards and above her. *'Excellent, tot. But beyond the particularities of every case, there is a shared stake. What is that?'* Their words rumbled with the ominous darkness of an engaged lecturer positing a tricky question. *'What are the stakes for the individual and the society alike?'*

Half-human-Áurea smirked savagely, savouring the word before speaking it. However, then-Áurea watched Élan with sleep-deprived eyes, pestered by the question that would lead to the answer she couldn't find.

To the mentor, both responses were simultaneous.

Long ago, and whispered anxiously, then-Áurea's answer was a non-answer but a sibilant question. "Who am I?"

Élan nodded, aware her question would eventually lead to the correct answer—the name of the most important alive element.

Now, confident regardless of her ignorance, half-human-Áurea dared to whisper, "Identity." She straightened almost proudly. "Political decay leads to the loss of political identity, which legitimises a ruler based on tenets perceived as shared. Those tenets shape a society's identity. Likewise, the shift in someone's mindset leads to the alteration of their *individual* identity."

Élan cawed in approval and soared to land on her awaiting shoulder.

Then-Áurea was drowning in unspoken questions, terrified of the alive elements she ought to manipulate as a Soul Transmuter. Meanwhile, half-human-Áurea was beginning to see their cross-cutting nature—even when more was needed for her to comprehend.

The raven glanced at both with a silver eye, mind-whispering, *'Tell me. What is identity?'*

Verve

5072-5074 CE

The dusk brought an uncluttered sky and a cluttered mind. A map of nascent stars but a labyrinth of ideas. A muffled and distant city, but a boisterous and animated search for an answer.

Amidst that quiet turmoil of thoughts, Verve transmuted into a seven-foot humanoid of smoke and alighted onto the greenhouse's glass rooftop. Glamouring to invisibility, they glanced inside with four ruby eyes—Iúrdan was trimming branches while singing a lullaby, half-hidden by the crown of a potted tree. He worked peacefully, collecting sap, plucking leaves, and harvesting flowers and herbs to later craft medicine.

The alchemist narrowed their eyes at the human. Iúrdan's shielding mindset was strong and uncommon—but he was wholly human and explainable, even if particularly resilient.

Metal clattered inside the greenhouse, and the healer's curses hiked to the sky, interrupting Verve's ruminations. They looked down again, watching as he collected his shears and pruners, his basket with weeds now tumbling through the floor. Verve cocked their head, perusing Iúrdan's alive elements as he cleaned the mess of branches and leaves—but their thoughts soon redirected to the enigma of The Rector's mission.

Still invisible, they waved a smoke-made hand, dripping soot and forcing the sound waves to remain inside the immediate area around the alchemist. In the renewed quietude, they lifted a palm up, remembering the leader's words and regenerating the sound waves of their voice. Enabled by this Protean ability, those echoes grew into a small circle, bumping and twisting to mimic the frequency of The Rector's voice.

"Go to Amberina and find Iúrdan. Study him; he is important to me," the commanding alchemist whispered again, that same cadence twisting like a riddle.

Another circle blossomed from Verve's memory, resounding with their own mind-voice. "What do I need to study?"

"The unexplainable," The Rector repeated, his circle thickening and thinning with their otherworldly cadence.

The Chimera-Warlord twitched their fingers, and the sound waves bounced back, repeating the words. After a moment's thought, the alchemist willed specific soundbites to split into smaller circles, each containing fragments of The Rector's commands.

"He is important to me." One clue to the riddle. Then, a second one. "He is a key." Another pause, another hint. "The unexplainable."

Two more soundbites split, one with Verve's modulated yet flat tone. "You are after knowledge. *What* knowledge?"

The Rector murmured again, muted. "Ground-breaking knowledge."

Lightning rippled around Verve, yet they reigned that half-alive element, strengthening their invisibility glamour. After a month of futile investigation, Verve had concluded that Iúrdan himself was *not* unexplainable, but something else was; something derived from his mindset, which was likely caused by his interaction with the patients. Through them, Verve surmised, Iúrdan could eventually think or feel something that may lead to ground-breaking knowledge.

After all, a human consciousness was a source of alive elements. Nothing else within them was worth studying.

A thousand new questions roared as Verve remained motionless, invisible, and clustered within a soundless bubble. Were The Rector's words metaphors? Or were they being purposefully, obtusely literal? What could be unexplainable? And more importantly, how did The Rector *detect* it? Or was the wording just a metaphor to indicate knowledge outside of Verve's grasp? Perhaps knowledge related to non-alive elements?

The alchemist pushed those questions away. This mission was clearly more convoluted than expected and it was too early to determine which questions were meaningful, and which just pointless pursuits comprehensible only to The Rector's unreachable mind. The only reasonable step forward was to define better experiments to test Iúrdan's shielding mindset... and given the basic approach taken for the past month, Verve gauged they had to become *imaginative*.

The soundbites were still echoing around them, yet Verve smothered them, instead looking down through the glass rooftop to follow Iúrdan with their gaze. Whatever they did had to guide them through their assortment of questions, to solve the riddle of The Rector's mission.

Verve observed as hundreds of patients passed by, juxtaposing ailments and reactions, and corroborating Iúrdan's commonality. His mental shield was ever-present, strengthened by a working schedule that stopped for nothing sans his sporadic errands to the market, his need to sleep and eat, and his nocturnal gardening.

For a few months, Verve found a variety of humans and produced smaller, less memorable experiments to determine any weaknesses. They soon confirmed that the genre, age, or appearance of a patient were so irrelevant to Iúrdan that he just considered them as a body with symptoms—even when his gentleness was praised in the town's region.

In that impasse, the alchemist also determined that the town's location had impacted Iúrdan's mind. Because of the proximity to the Forest of Cortezas, there was no shortage of hunters wounded by wolves, bears, or fellow humans, nor of unfortunate travellers stabbed by thieves. To Verve, those natural occurrences were a futile waste of human resources, since Iúrdan's inner peace was attuned to protect him from those cases; the process was repetitious, and soon the alchemist stopped documenting those cases. The only curiosity was the aftermath, when the healer would rapidly process the events into a list of lessons learned and depleted supplies, showcasing an uncommon ability to dehumanise the memory of his patients.

Yet beyond that peaceful mindset and his irrefutable schedule, another constant was Iúrdan's work on his greenhouse.

Some days, he watered and pruned the trees, while others he weeded and potted plants, fertilising the soil or hunting vermin. To Verve's dismay, he sang lullabies to the plants with the same gentleness he applied to the patients, falling into an idle, contented peace—yet again, the alchemist only found common, human-like reactions. Methods meant to cope with misery; leisure activities meant to brighten the soul-link with embers of relief and comfort.

In those days, the alchemist couldn't avoid thinking that if a Chimera-Warlord had to complete this mission, Hellion—with their affinity to plants and spores—seemed a more suitable choice... except that, as Verve had thought during their conversation with The Rector, the leader was anything but haphazard in their decision making.

Other days, Iúrdan arrived with lists of recipes only to spend hours crafting complex and convoluted blends, both for specific patients or to restock his supplies. Verve found those lists interesting because the blends were too advanced for the region... but also because those tasks exploited his analytical thinking. It deprived the soul-link of any emotion except the thoughtful repetition of crafting steps, weighed amounts, and observed reactions.

Yet passive as those months were for the alchemist, they were all carefully planned.

Verve observed, always invisible, always looming over, always soul-linking the healer to scavenge the depths of his conscious and unconscious alive elements. From that connection, they distilled facts, weaving a network of evidence to establish commonalities, study the subject, and determine what experiment could reveal the unexplained. After gathering enough details, they found a pattern and a weakness.

The pattern was the known use of rationalisation applied to cope with extreme emotions. Iúrdan lived by his profession, and everything in his life revolved around actively tending to patients or completing tasks that enabled him to do so. To the alchemist, such focus exposed him to never-ending grief and suffering, to loss and sorrow, and to guilt and regret—and after a lifetime of exposure, the healer had developed the fearless apathy caused by comprehending that risk and uncertainty were as inevitable as death—and its prospect no longer triggered the extreme reactions fear could cause.

The weakness was caused by that very same fearless apathy, and its dependence on the *known*. When many patients believed in myths and curses to explain what they ignored, the healer worked to unearth the logical cause of the ailment to produce a logical solution.

After pondering those facts and clues, on one starry night, Verve settled on a new experiment. It had to rely on something irrational, possible but not quite, suspicious but just so—even for the healer. They would be imaginative, but the result would certainly expedite the mission.

Transmuted into a strand of silvery smoke, Verve slipped through the slivers of a window, glamouring to invisibility. Iúrdan's chambers were small and functional, outfitted with a rack of well-worn clothes, a stool that doubled as a table for a lantern, and a rickety bed that barely supported his weight.

He sprawled on it, one arm crossing over his chest, the other dangling over the edge. The sheet slid with every intake of breath, slowly uncovering his loincloth. His snoring interrupted the soft whizzing of the wind, and when he turned, the bed creaked as loudly as the cart shrieking on the road outside. Horses neighed in distress, and desperate voices shouted to one another—but the sleeping healer snored, oblivious.

Verve soul-linked him, marvelling at the profound, dreamless sleep that blocked sound waves as effectively as Protean alchemy.

"'ealer!!" A woman screeched outside, voice deep but strained by fear.

Her curses vanished in the night, and heavy knocking hammered the house's door. Verve caught the sound, forcing it to bounce in the marble doors, magnifying the echo to thunder into the bedroom. The healer jolted to sit on his creaking bed, eyes wide open, soul-link heavy with his confusion and over-whelmed senses.

"Iúrdan, open up!!" A man bellowed, panting and knocking again. "Iúrdan! 'elp!!"

That plea spurn him into action. He scrambled to the clothes rack, put on his trousers before retrieving the lantern, and ran barefoot through his house; Verve followed closely, invisible and focused on the soul-link. With every stumble and every breath, Iúrdan's mind cleared of confusion, progressing into the calm state he favoured during emergencies.

"I'm coming!!" Iúrdan shouted back, slipping on the polished marble floor while struggling with the lantern's mechanism. It clicked, and a small flame sparked inside the glass container. "Coming!!!"

The healer slammed against the front door, single-handedly wrestling with the lock. It clicked open, and he backtracked to watch the man outside. He was young, with sun-kissed skin, a broken nose, and long blonde hair. His hunting clothes were grimy, and fresh blood spattered from his chest down, fabric soaked and dripping. Iúrdan frowned, noticing the huntress tying the horses' reins to a post while his thousand hypotheses swarmed the soul-link—until someone moaned from the cart, startling him. He ran, dashing across the frontal garden, rounding on the cart, and bending to uncover the wounded man.

Verve was following the healer when uncertainty and disbe-lief blasted through the soul-link like recharged lightning, shocking Iúrdan's mind. For a moment, the alchemist observed as the healer etched his gaze on the patient's right leg while thinking of nothing. It was severed too cleanly, sliced too perfectly, cut at an impossible angle—low outside, but higher on the inner tight.

For a few heartbeats, the soul-link remained vacant and barren, devoid of thoughts even when his sight provided the irrefutable evidence of the illogical. Verve absorbed this emptiness, disassembling it into shock, perplexity, apprehension, suspicion, and uneasiness before adding it to their network of evidence and clues. In the fifth heartbeat, Iúrdan blinked, mumbling while his mind swung between aversion and terror—and Verve devoured that information, weaving it into their grid.

In his tenth hammering heartbeat, the healer's reasoning sparked within him like thunder roaring through a hailstorm. It amused the alchemist, who swirled around while Iúrdan issued cold and calculated commands, ushering the pair of stunned hunters to react. His orders were flat and firm, commanding and convincing even when only doubt and indecision danced through the soul-link—a detail that delighted the alchemist. He sent broken-nose for water, asked the huntress for help, and began a tortuous, gory meandering to carry the wounded man.

As they moved, Verve focused on the soul-link. It resonated with what little Iúrdan heard of the huntress' spluttered explanation, and his own thought-voice, shouting his diagnosis to smother any emotional interference.

"Somet'eng cut Peiro. We were in thuh forest." The huntress, mumbling.

Severe blood loss. Must bind the vessels. Iúrdan, already imagining the procedure.

"Out of noth'eng. 'is leg. A blink. It was gone." The huntress, panicking, dragging her friend.

The bone. Cleanly sliced, no shards. Like the trousers. Iúrdan, sliding in the corner and regaining his balance. *Clean and cauterise immediately. No time left.*

"Thuh *wind* cut Peiro! It c–cursed us and wounded 'im!" Broken-nose. Somewhere inside the house. "Sodd'eng lanterns!"

"We were eat'eng, camp'eng. T–there was a noise; thuh… thuh wind *whispered* 'ateful words. I 'eard it." The huntress, huffing while helping lay Peiro on the bed.

Clammy, cold skin. Shallow breathing. Weak pulse. Iúrdan, seeking his wrist, before ripping his pants.

"I'll find thuh wife!" Broken-nose, stomping out of the clinic.

Still riding the wind, Verve slipped into the room like invisible smoke, alighting onto the farthest table near a cupboard. Rolling to a corner, they focused on the soul-link while the healer dashed from one cupboard to another. He fetched items so intuitively that each concept blurred in his unconscious, vanishing after he dropped them on the stool near the patient's bed.

His reactions were so instinctive that Verve wondered whether the healer had embedded the knowledge into his identity, or if the previous shock had pierced his mental shield. Either case elicited the alchemist's curiosity, and once they added those observations into their network, they focused on the healer's action.

Methodically, Iúrdan wrestled a cushioned wooden roll into the man's mouth, uncorking a bottle to rain vinegar over the stump. The huntress shrieked, and Peiro moaned, contorting—but the healer bound his limbs to the bed with leather straps. Then he tightened the tourniquet above the stump, ignoring the moans. Soaking the scalpels, he ignited the heater and pushed two blades into the flames. His gaze drifted back to the wound, and his analytical prowess returned tenfold.

Through their connection, Verve saw through his eyes, coexisting in the same vacuousness devoid of thoughts and handled by impulses. The pair detected the blood vessels, classified them by risk, and noted the edges of the nerves—and then it faded, leaving the alchemist to peruse a mindless and insensitive soul-link.

In that moment, Iúrdan neglected any leaden reasoning for the agility of instinct and the momentum of experience. He was meticulous and efficient, burning blood vessels with a heated scalpel and replacing the blade on the heater. It was so deliberate and rigorous that Verve studied him, submerged in that abyssal thoughtlessness while unable to add any observation to their network of evidence.

In that moment, Peiro exhaled and relaxed, head falling back while the huntress wailed and screamed. Iúrdan dropped the scalpels to compress the man's chest, but through his reaction, Verve noticed a nuance they had never uncovered during those seven months of observations.

Iúrdan was producing no alive elements.

Verve reviewed the soul-link, increasingly baffled each time —but their conclusion was irrefutable.

The healer didn't think while removing the wooden piece from Peiro's mouth, nor felt anything when rolling his head— mouth foaming—to the side. He commanded the huntress with a flat tone and compressed Peiro's chest with the mechanical precision of a Machina's contraption. When the hunter's heart reignited, Iúrdan paused his motions, grabbing his locked wrist to count.

The need to further the experiment overwhelmed Verve, and they soul-shaped the wounded man. Magnifying the broken shards of his remaining alive-elements, the alchemist mind-whispered a deadly command, *'Stop breathing.'*

On cue, Peiro widened his eyes, gaping without breathing. Iúrdan noticed immediately, reviewing his mouth and resuming the compressions—but even as that heart stopped, the healer's mind remained devoid of alive elements.

Verve disposed of the second soul-link, refocusing on the healer even when his mind was as blank as the dead man's— again corroborating the oddest observation ever seen.

Iúrdan felt no sorrow, no guilt, no misery. He did not review his actions nor regretted them. Instead, he watched the hunter, sighing and stopping himself before pinching his own nose with a bloodied hand. Swiping the left to close Peiro's eyes, he rounded on the bed, turned off the heater and barely glanced at the wound before aiming for the huntress.

"Peiro!?" A woman shrieked in the waiting room. "Peiro!!"

She screeched mournfully, startling the quiet emptiness of Iúrdan's soul-link. She dashed inside, slumping over the body. For a moment, Verve considered soul-shaping the wife to produce another reaction, but Iúrdan's gentle voice convinced them otherwise.

He was patting her back, moving her hair, and speaking in a

reassuring cadence—yet while he spoke, his reasoning reappeared so shattered and sporadic that Verve restarted the soul-link a few times, utterly confused.

That Chimerical ability, often blindingly nuanced, yielded no more details than their natural perception of alive elements. Iúrdan's thoughts were loose words bouncing in his mind, and his emotions were a dull approximation of the generic, primal feelings. Shame, when guilt and remorse would've been more appropriate, and muted fear instead of apprehension. A dash of sadness instead of sorrow, and a mote of anger in lieu of outrage.

Soaring to will a faint breeze, Verve swirled around the room, unable to define the experiment as a success or a failure.

Iúrdan's lack of alive elements was even more unusual than his professional self-control—and Verve explained it through the healer's extreme detachment born from the sheer need of mental self-preservation. It further evidenced his disregard of risk and uncertainty, muting down his desire to help to avoid the heartbreak and misery brought by losing a patient... but there was something quaint about that lack.

As Verve's wind ululated through the patient's room, chilling the huntress and spreading the odour of burnt flesh, a realisation dawned on them.

Instead of emptying the soul-link, that *lack* had saturated it with *nothingness*.

Nothingness was, to the alchemist, an absurd qualifier for a preposterous situation both obnoxiously amusing and excitingly frustrating. An improbable event seldom documented, an exception, and likely another piece in the puzzle of that mission. The case of a working human consciousness that had—temporarily—produced no alive elements, then issuing fragmented, shattered thoughts while remaining functional, and somehow saturating the soul-link.

Nothingness was, as Verve soon learned, the distant end of a road riddled with reasonable hypotheses and failed experiments.

Verve's first theory, soon after Peiro's death, had been straightforward—to create cases edging between factual reality and unproven myths, to gauge Iúrdan's reactions. The alchemist's original reasoning had also been straightforward—the healer was too logical, too agnostic, too rational. He worked with proven theories and knowledge, discarding beliefs and faith; therefore, witnessing evidence of a myth could have been a likely cause.

Yet after four months of thorough observation and unique experiments, Verve rejected the first hypothesis. Those maimed, mutilated humans had been as memorable as Piero's, but timed and spaced out not to damage the healer's unexplainable mind. Measured not to start a myth that could stir too much curiosity and hinder The Orders' pursuit of knowledge.

All wasteful failures.

None reproduced the nothingness nor broke the healer's soul-link. None clued the alchemist nor plunged Iúrdan into that unusual mindset.

Nothingness became, to Verve, a faulty label assigned to an observation oddly devoid of itself. A sequence of abstract goals —to reproduce, to observe, to study—surrounding the puzzle of their mission. A fortuitous event that would remain so until reproduced.

Verve's second theory required three months to prepare— whatever the ailment was, the patient had to wither and die painfully, while their relatives witnessed the decay. The alchemist's reasoning was that such inherent hopelessness and misery would trigger another of Iúrdan's coping strategies, resulting in that nothingness.

These four cases required a few months of preparation, but arrived in pairs—by chance for the humans, yet as per the alchemist's schedule. An overpowering allergy, a consuming tumour, a degeneration that deformed and disabled the victim, and an unpredictable weakness that seized a youngster. All gradual and unavoidable. Painful for the body, and taxing for the mind.

As certain as the fact that Verve—one way or another—would reproduce that nothingness in their pursuit of knowledge.

Where the first hypothesis had presented unexpected situations demanding extreme yet short-term concentration, the second brought something different. Foreseeable, meandering, and dreadful situations that nurtured the deepest misery and the darkest fears of the involved humans, coating their existence with the unavoidable truth of death's inevitability.

Exactly as Verve had predicted, Iúrdan took care of them, as gentle and attentive as with any other sufferer. He treated the fated patients and the grievous relatives, soothing the former and preparing the latter to mourn and heal.

Slowly, with every day passing in that clinic, and every night invested in the greenhouse, Iúrdan's thoughts changed.

"Death is natural. Struggle is natural," he whispered every night after their visits, stretched on the lectus in his greenhouse. "Easing their pain is all I can do."

His thoughts repeated, emotionless like incessant revisions of symptoms, quotes and extracts from papyrus, lists of herbs and analytical rows of hypothetical, palliative concoctions. But that *nothingness*, that lack that once saturated his mind, that coveted outcome, did not return. To Verve's dismay, Iúrdan's soul-link showcased nothing different from the healer's normal mindset.

"Death is natural. Struggle is natural," Iúrdan kept whispering, every night spent on the greenhouse, every moment while crafting more medicine. "Death is natural. Death is…"

After seven more months of incurable patients arriving, decaying, and dying, Verve rejected their second hypothesis. Those experiments, those wilting humans, had only plunged the healer into a variant of his normal mindset, and the alchemist into a stagnation caused by uncertainty.

In that stalemate, Verve deemed that two unacceptable perils were banning their progress. If they attempted more experiments, they risked damaging the healer's mind; on the contrary, if they continued to watch, they would risk the human dying, or stagnating without producing any results.

Normality ensued as the alchemist debated over their options and, slowly, Iúrdan's soul-link began to oscillate between the quietude of not thinking and the vacuum blocking any feelings. Peace, amidst the daily tasks in the greenhouse, with those embers of relief and comfort swirling around. Apathy, surrounding the patients and their treatment, yet hidden beneath a layer of politeness and pretence.

Amidst that boring uniformity of the healer's life, the alchemist finally decanted for one of those risks.

Verve's third theory appealed to a sickness of the mind that caused no visible effects on the body—something invisible except to the sufferer that would likely require months to brew. Therefore, after identifying the next three subjects, and through a handful of months, Verve soul-shaped their minds with overwhelming emotions—unreasonable panic, unsustainable gloominess, and mind-churning anxiety. Those patients arrived on precisely chosen days. The first on a common, tedious day of issuing medicine and simple symptoms. The second, amidst an exuberant sequence of gory accidents and wailing patients. The third, in the middle of the market while procuring food and supplies.

To Verve's frustration, Iúrdan's response was unexpected. His soul-link immersed into the unpredictable alternation of two mental states, neither resembling whatever Peiro had caused, nor supporting the alchemist's latest hypothesis.

Half of Iúrdan's thought patterns were so detached and logical that his reasoning reshaped into vivid, real-time transcriptions that clogged Verve's soul-link—and through that nuance, they uncovered a small and irrelevant fact. Iúrdan, emotionally distant and apathetic, did not care for his patients, instead acting because of his blind duty to his profession.

The other half of Iúrdan's thought patterns manifested peace. It dulled his anguish, forgetting and forgiving his failure to heal them because, unless he ignored those feelings, he would trade his own sanity for his patients' unachievable well-being.

"Death is natural. Struggle is natural," he whispered, repetitious.

Two years after arriving, Verve rejected their last hypothesis, accepting that failure was an inherent part of research—but they stood in the greenhouse's corner, invisible and soured by the impossibility of reproducing that remarkable nothingness.

The sky stained cobalt, aubergine and plum, with pink edging the double silver suns—one near the skyline, the other slightly above. The colours of lightning framed the sunset, slipping through the greenhouse's glass ceiling and reflecting on the plants beneath. Their leaves took on ethereal colours, with slivers of pinks and violets, enthralling enough to distract the healer from his gardening.

He was kneeling near a flowerbed, pruners held haphazardly in one hand, mouth slightly agape and eyes lost in a bush. After a few idle moments, Iúrdan inhaled its scent, humming approvingly, and resumed his pruning with a pleased countenance. He alternated between mumbling and humming a lullaby, occasionally interrupted with a groan or another thoughtful noise.

Verve observed him from atop the glass rooftop, glamoured to invisibility to hide their humanoid smoke-made form—but his soul-link was, as usual, a pointless connection that yielded nothing else than his embers of relief and contentment. The frustration of unsatisfied curiosity rippled through them, compelling the clouds to reflect their mood—slowly streaking the sky, aiming for the sunset but failing to reach it.

Two years of rejecting hypotheses had passed by, disappointing but riveting, frustrating but fascinating. Two years to observe a single phenomenon, while failing all attempts to reproduce it. Two years in which Verve wove questions into a looping circle of uncertainty, only to settle on the obvious; the nothingness was the unexplainable... but how to define it? How to explain it?

The sky rumbled in tandem with the alchemist's reasoning, darkening as a storm brewed in the sky and in their mind—but a whimper resonated inside the greenhouse, punctuated by rattling metal and loud enough to interrupt Verve's thunderous theorisation.

Iúrdan was sucking on his forefinger, a drop of blood trickling down his hand, a sickle lying on the floor. Arrows of pain darted from him as he meandered back to the cupboard to wrap that finger before returning to work. His pain endured in the back of his mind while he tended to the pots, again falling into his peaceful state. His contented, polychromatic embers faded into transparent shapes, and his mind lulled into a flatness that purposefully disregarded any thought, letting go of whatever transitory idea crossed his mind.

To the alchemist, Iúrdan's motions were too ingrained after decades of gardening—yet too different from that *nothingness* seen during Peiro's experiment.

The one caused by a moment in which a living human had produced no alive elements, followed by a mental state so shattered—yet somehow functional and rational—that Verve had considered their soul-link to be flawed.

Verve narrowed their crimson eyes at the healer, considering an alchemical truth—humans, as a source of alive elements, were unreliable. Millenniums of alchemical research demonstrated that mind-wounds, and the successive experience of extreme or atemporal emotions, could damage a consciousness. When that happened, the wounded person only produced erratic alive elements or, in the worst cases, none at all; humans at those extremes were not functional.

Therefore, the alchemist concluded, their choice of words was incorrect. *Nothingness* was a flawed word to approximate an unusual phenomenon, likely misleading their approach since Peiro's death. Melting their humanoid body, the alchemist transmuted into tendrils of smoke, and allowed themselves to posit a new hypothesis.

What if that *nothingness* did not imply that Iúrdan was not producing alive elements? What if it was, instead, a gap filled by something undetectable? Something that exhibited different intensities? After all, alive elements had innate intensities that blended from subtle to staggering; while fear oscillated between tenuous apprehension and abject terror, desire existed between coy interest and inordinate craving.

Tracking the healer with part of their mind, Verve used their seemingly viable idea to dare another. If the nothingness had intensities, then it was quite possible that, for almost eighteen months, they had attempted—and failed—to produce the most extreme version of something yet unexplainable.

Annoyed at such oversight, Verve further theorised that Iúrdan's normal mind-state was, in actuality, the weakest form of that nothingness... in which case they had spent months witnessing *it* while unaware they were doing so. Therefore, that *gap*, that thoughtlessness-to-nothingness spectrum could be a variant of a known alive element, or a new alive element—either shrouded from Verve but not missing from Iúrdan.

As the double suns chased each other towards the horizon, there was only quietude—but Verve's will exploded towards the sky, coercing the charges in the clouds. They burst, amethyst and azure, lightning slithering luminously to thunder in under-standing. The dusk was dead, murdered by the emotional storm assailing the alchemist.

Desire for whatever new knowledge The Rector was after. Ambition for whatever it could imply for Verve. Elation for wherever this would take The Orders. Knowledge; the blissful goal no alchemist could ever achieve, doomed to endlessly chase it. Greed, for—

Iúrdan groaned loudly, looking up and scowling at the glass ceiling while unknowingly interrupting the alchemist. He mumbled in annoyance, contorting to watch the sudden storm —and the motion calmed the alchemist, easing the wind's whistling and returning them to the consideration of cold facts.

Verve's obsession with reproducing an unconventional phenomenon had misled them into failed experiments derived from misconstrued hypotheses—now unsustainable if they considered that the nothingness—the gap—existed within a spectrum of intensities. Therefore, the only viable approach was to observe without interfering, to gather enough information, and to let Iúrdan's shrouded alive elements to flare.

5074-5077 CE

Identity. A question asked multiple times, receiving different answers from each Áurea.

A complex concept. A mirage-made cage. A set of epithets aiming to narrow a fluid, ever-evolving notion. A construct influenced and judged by everyone and everything. An idea as undefinable as ostracising.

In reality, it was an intricate alive element at the centre of Élan's grid of lectures. One created by individuals and groups alike, one whose manipulation often changed the course of history.

Yet more was needed before her identity could be breached, and so Élan wove lessons across time and space, always guiding the mentee to evolve. When the more basic concepts cleared, when all Áureas understood what alive elements were—mental states, thought patterns, emotions—only then the raven-alchemist wove in a new type of lectures.

One meant to destroy, ravage, and reshape identity.

Ultimately, then-Áurea needed to forget hers for half-human-Áurea to find theirs.

"Such a tricky question," then-Áurea asked, struggling to keep up the pace behind her mentor. "Identity is one's definition of the self."

The raven cawed, disapproving. *'Too vague, tot,'* they shrilled, melting into shadows. *'You need to comprehend it to transfigure yourself.'*

By sheer will, the alchemist coaxed the room to reveal their latest prey—the one captured as a medium for the new lecture. The space reacted to that command, and the starlight-ridden floor rippled like water as a human figure emerged upwards. She was gagged, her legs roped together, and her arms bound behind her back.

Then-Áurea waned at the sight, pointing a trembling finger to the terrorised woman of rose-gold locks lying on the ground.

"She's here, not like the others beneath the glass floor! Why is she here?" Her lips trembled with a thousand questions; her scowl quieted a thousand more. "Who is she!?"

'You ask the same of you. Frequently, as of late,' Élan answered directly to the mentee's mind.

To the alchemist, all Áureas were asking the right questions —but her understanding of identity remained superficial. Nothing more than the mindless repetition of words whose individual meaning was understandable, but whose combination rendered only an abstract idea. Such intuition was not enough; neither for a transfiguration or to advance in alchemy. Identity was at the core of a Soul Transmuter's abilities.

Therefore, Élan had set the stage to shatter Áurea's self enough to enable her progress—whether or not she understood it. Then-Áurea had to morph, to advance, to improve. To vanish. The Rector had ordered it, and Élan would achieve it with this lesson.

"Élan, tell me, who is *she!?*" Then-Áurea whined again, so fixed in the captive she didn't notice the shadows moving.

Sneaking their tendrils, the alchemist throttled the captive and bound the mentee—creeping through her legs, curling through her body and immobilising her in place. She barely whelped, accustomed to the process, and Élan leveraged the moment to mind-yoke then-Áurea. That alchemical skill turned her into a mere observer; a consciousness devoid of autonomy and forced to experience the mentor's alchemy.

'*Scavenge her.*' Élan ordered, eager to fulfil The Rector's command—and perhaps fathom their plans. '*Tell me who she is.*'

The order was still echoing in then-Áurea's mind when the alchemist amalgamated the captive woman. An amalgamation was a fatal binding of a being's identity to a Chimera's will, and Élan used it to slice open the captive's alive elements, spreading them into pieces and feeding them to Áurea through the mind-yoke. It wouldn't last long, just enough for Áurea to learn—amalgamations destroyed the victim's body once the minds were dissolved.

'*Find the answer to your question,*' the mentor demanded again. '*Who is she?*'

Élan unleashed a dam of foreign memories from the captive, Talesa[1], sinking then-Áurea in otherness.

Complacency, quietude. The pointless laughter of ballrooms and wine, of the bland jolliness of richness, of the comfortable life of nobility. Envy, now petty and nonsensical, then imperative and urgent—for dresses and jewellery, for youth and beauty. Those were all memories, stained with the present regret that had revised and corrected them, mourned and buried them.

Long ago, Talesa had been a noblewoman, a philanthropist, a wife, a mother. Now, that was an unspeakable past. A lifestyle that had been, but that would never be again. Suddenly, another of Talesa's emotions sliced through those memories. Despair. It unleashed terror and grief, recalling that civil war that delivered Talesa a spike with her husband's head and a chest with her children's limbs.

Then-Áurea did not react, so shocked she was by the barrage of foreign emotions—but Élan wouldn't stop; they needed a reaction. Therefore, through the amalgamation, the alchemist scavenged Talesa's emotions, passing them to the mentee to experience.

Betrayal and misery, disgust and loneliness, desire for what

---

1. Read as /ta'lesa/ (TAH-**LEH**-SAH).

had been, and reproach for the foolish, overly-simplistic view of the past. In contrast, her present was a vacuum. Everything that made Talesa herself had been taken away; there was no corpse to mourn, no time to cry, no ruins where to return. What was she, without the balls, without the jewels? What was she, without her contacts, now as dead and mangled as her loved ones?

Finally, then-Áurea gagged and Élan nudged her emotions to mingle with Talesa's. Through the enduring connection, they felt her past misery, the nights spent awake in numbing hopelessness, that mind-eating void so filled with questions she couldn't answer.

"Who am I!?" Talesa and Áurea screamed. One silenced by the amalgamation, the other by the mind-yoke—both equally powerless.

'You tell me,' Élan mind-whispered, strengthening the mind-yoke as Talesa's screams overpowered Áurea's. 'That is exactly what you need to answer.'

The mentee fell to her knees, mouth wide open. She only gulped, mumbling, nails sinking into her cheeks.

Amidst and beyond the amalgamation, the pain became intangible yet real, unphysical yet ravaging; so truthful that both women relieved it in unison. That alive element floated between them, encompassing the room, as Élan willed the mind-yoke to transfer more of it—until, because of that pain, there was only darkness.

Nothingness. Absolute apathy clogged the barren casket of a body that looked like Talesa but wasn't her. Long ago, the misery and grief had permanently altered the construct of her identity; now, because of the amalgamation, that deconstruction happened again. It walked through empty roads, like Áurea had done. It cried in silence because their numbed minds could only swim in grief for themselves; for who they were before. Each retaken step chipped Talesa-Áurea away, banning memories, blanking thoughts, blocking regrets.

At that moment, Talesa-Áurea questioned everything. "Who am I?" Homeless. "Who am I?" Betrayed. "Who am I!?" Depressed, miserable. "What am I?" Meaningless, hollow.

'*Finally!*' Élan chuckled, delighted by the switch. 'What *is the correct question, tot!*'

Encouraged by Áurea's change, the alchemist ransacked Talesa's alive elements, tearing her apart through the amalgamation. They flung thoughts of destitution and scoured rhetorical questions, rummaging through ingrained feelings while disassembling Talesa's identity into pieces simple enough for Áurea to comprehend.

'*Stop anthropomorphising yourself, tot. A Soul Transmuter's identity is more than that! Here, use this memory...*' they stated, rippling as they found what they needed.

A thought. A light at the end of the tunnel of Talesa's numbness.

"I need to reinvent myself," the captive had spoken once, but the words echoed now amidst the amalgamation—stained crimson and flowing like the blood pouring through the floor.

Élan ignored the carmine river. What was a dying human—or a few!—in the greater scheme of training a Soul Transmuter? One useful to no other than The Rector? With reignited curiosity, the alchemist reinforced the mind-yoke, swirling Talesa's idea to Áurea. The mentee bellowed in misery, strangled physically and mentally—and only because she'd been in a similar situation once, but on the road to The Towers.

"I can change. I can... try," Talesa had spoken once, when begging a baker to take her in. The plea echoed now through the amalgam, revisited like thoughts.

"I will change," past-Áurea had muttered, when departing Strezia's palace.

"Who—?" then-Áurea stammered in that obsidian room, choked by spitting blood. "Who... *was* she?"

'*Excellent!*' The mentor cackled, expanding the amalgamation. That was the precise realisation he craved; the moment for then-Áurea to be left behind. '*Was! Was! Was! Perfect!*'

Eager for a result, Élan willed the amalgamation to open, laying out every one of Talesa's thought patterns and emotions —and hurled those alive elements as they would hurl books at the Library. All Áureas read them like journals, desperate to learn the nuances brought by the captive's perspective.

'What now? What now!?' The mentor dared her, like a teacher scavenging the answer deeply hidden in a pupil's mind. *'Find the answer, tell me! What was she!?'*

Then-Áurea perused everything, pulling the alive elements apart to crack their basis, feel the memories, and label the causes. One by one, Talesa's alive elements—thought patterns, emotions, and mental states—melted into minimal, simplistic specks that fed another Áurea's alchemical knowledge, enabling a new iteration of the mentee.

But Talesa choked, dying as her body collapsed. Then-Áurea gargled with the captive's blood, the liquid filling her lungs as the questions-answers bubbled out of her.

"Not… yet!" Air, missing. "Live! I want… to live!" Life, fading. "No! Not that! I have… so much… more—to be!!" Time, fleeting. "Life. Not really. Not anymore!!" Desire, expiring the old remaining ideas and exposing the new ones. "I exist!!"

Élan halted the amalgamation, releasing the tendrils and stopping the mind-yoke. Talesa's body had shattered alongside her identity, and in the aftermath, her remnants were nothing more than shredded skin and broken limbs. The alchemist hopped between the streams of blood, morphing into the raven to alight near the mentee.

She was on all fours, fists hammering the starlight-ridden floor. Blood spattered in front of her, red and purple, but crystalline where her tears fell. Her braid was unmade, and her deep black coils now blended with rose-gold locks, cascading down her back and mingling with a few silvery feathers.

Stretching to watch her askance, Élan mind-whispered, tricky, *'Who are you?'*

Past-Áurea had shrugged, "Your mentee."

Then-Áurea had stuttered, "I don't know."

The initial half-human-Áurea coughed, spitting red-purple blood. "Not… *who*." She shook her head, rose-gold-black locks falling to her shoulders. "Who is what I was. Áurea. The poor human girl who became a Nova Noble, the middle-aged woman who left Strezia."

'Interesting.' Élan's curiosity bounced into the mentee's mind. They beckoned with a wing for emphasis. *'So, what are you?'*

Áurea chuckled, sitting on her heels and rubbing the blood out of her mouth. "Alive. Determined," she remarked, gaze fixed on Élan's. "Now, I live. But I will exist."

'What a change in attitude,' the raven cackled, amused. *'And such an important alive element.'*

A pathway, a thought pattern. Enduring yet flexible. It limited cognition, it narrowed feelings, it prescribed behaviours.

Élan taught, and all Áureas learned differently. Past-Áurea was too swarmed by questions, too shocked by the alchemist's nature. Then-Áurea was biased by the intrinsic morality required by time-framed, limited humans. Half-human-Áurea was refined, almost frameless, yet also biased.

But bias was a lesson that wouldn't come yet.

In the meantime, Élan strengthened the lectures, bringing back the debates—at another level, more nuanced and abstract than before.

'What is it? Attitude,' Élan wondered, philosophical. *'You had one, but now you have another one.'*

Amidst the Library, one less-human-Áurea chuckled, subversive. "At an individual level, attitude can lead to self-destruction or self-preservation. It's an enabler, and a required condition for existence itself." She paused, glancing over her feathered shoulder, arms spread open while she swirled the books hooked to her mind-stretch. "At a societal level, attitude is fundamental to strengthening peace. How the masses confront change, how they endure hardship, how they challenge a decaying or an established political construct... all of that depends on it."

Élan jolted into another table, positing questions for all Áureas to answer.

Yet amidst the atemporality of The Towers, the raven-bodied alchemist noticed a change. They cocked their head to watch less-human-Áurea askance—she was taller, ageless, pouting while a metal-coated finger toyed pensively with a rose-gold-black lock.

The moment they had once sowed had finally returned.

'I see you pouting. Why?' Élan asked for the third and last time. *'Did you find the underlying factor?'*

Less-human-Áurea waved her hand, palm up, forefinger swirling at nothing in particular. "Fear, as usual," she whispered, trailing off. "Fear of change, for whatever that change is. Desire as well, for numerous material or immaterial things. Everything can be summarised as fear and desire."

The raven cawed, shadows melting and expanding into a grin so wide it swallowed them. *'Elaborate, tot. Are you implying that only two emotions are fundamental?'*

She nodded, pensive. "Love, joy, and sadness are consequences of a fulfilled or unfulfilled desire, respectively. Surprise and anger are two reactions derived from a blend of fear and desire," less-human-Áurea paused, frowning in silence.

Élan swallowed their ambition, their intrigue about The Rector's command, and their insatiable curiosity just to focus on her. They soul-linked the mentee, only to witness how she unfurled emotions into their most basic layer by sheer knowledge; with logic and reasoning, translating intuition into words clear enough to be explained.

The alchemist waited patiently as she thought, marvelled by her thought patterns—and when she clicked her fingers, realisation smoothed her features, brightening the soul-link.

"Fear and desire lead to conservatism," less-human-Áurea stated, pinching her chin. "An individual yearns to keep a state, even if horrific or abusive, just for fear of the unknown and a desire for stability. A society does the same, and thus they all undergo political decay," she rumbled, so thoughtful that her words became thoughts. A breath after, she was mind-whispering instead of talking. *'That conservatism leads to frustration since the individual or the society fear the current state could worsen and hence desire something better.'*

'Thus fear and desire alternate, causing other emotions. Likewise, the blend of feelings forces humans to decide on whether to support the

status quo, with all its negative traits, or risk revolution,' the mentor added, melting their raven body into shadow tendrils. *'But what is attitude, then?'*

'The set of emotions and behaviours towards something caused by fear and desire,' less-human-Áurea gasped, clapping lightly as realisation dawned on her. *'And just like all alive elements, attitude is non-linear. Atemporal. What someone experiences before continues now or ahead, regardless of the interruption. They simply need the tiniest reminder, the smallest comment from a peer, and the long-forgotten attitude will return to the forefront.'*

Through the continuing soul-link, Élan felt the alive elements weaving through the mentee, reshaping her perceptions, and tugging her towards the possibility of a transfiguration.

'An accurate observation,' the alchemist confirmed, delighted by the improvement and eager for more answers. *'But what happens when an old attitude returns and remains?'*

'Everything stalls. A government, a society, a person...' Less-human-Áurea's mind-whisper mellowed as the words slowed, embittered. She clicked her tongue, grimacing and muttering, "The rolling shift between progress and pause enables evolution. The continuance of any… ensures stagnation."

The mentor's shadow ringlets crept through her arms, coiling over her shoulder to morph into the raven. *'Quite so, tot. But what soured you?'*

"I'm stagnating," half-human-Áurea recognised, standing in the Empty Room. "I hate this. I was advancing. Changing."

'Stagnation is the root of all hate. Towards oneself and others,' Élan answered once.

However, within The Towers, the lessons continued in all timelines.

Past-Áurea replied, still human in body, slowly evolving in mind. "It's death; the lack of change. It creeps slowly, devouring itself until only two shadows remain. One, the desire to be as before, and two, the fear of rotting entirely," she seethed, while painstakingly tearing one page apart.

'*Indeed, stagnation kills the mind. It leads to war and disorder,*' the mentor confirmed to all Áureas.

It didn't matter when or to whom; time was irrelevant within The Towers.

Past-Áurea scowled. She was still bursting with unspoken questions, still stunned and humbled by the alchemical elements. "In that case, change is *life*. You adapt or die. Mentally or physically," she spat, clicking her tongue while her fists clenched. "That's why I left Strezia. That's why I'm here. To change. To reinvent myself."

'*You're making excuses, relying on past choices. Neither matters to what you are now,*' Élan stated repeatedly, simultaneously, emphatically—yet always didactic, observational.

"I'm not! I'm simply remembering why I'm here," past-Áurea grunted, half-whining like the tot she was.

Somewhen, then-Áurea continued the conversation, pensive and introspective. "Maybe I'm just... afraid of existing without the revenge that fuels me."

This time, half-human-Áurea shrugged, the feathers on her shoulder rustling as she talked. "Nothing matters except existing. And the gap between my current life and my desired existence... terrifies me."

Further ahead, less-human-Áurea mind-whispered, '*Those excuses were a goal once and mattered long ago. That is a fact, therefore they matter, regardless of the timeline.*' She spread her fingers, watching her lilac-spotted walnut skin. '*Although my current goals differ, my identity remains the biggest obstacle.*'

Élan cawed four times, once to each Áurea—admonishing, patient, intrigued, approving.

'*That's why we alchemists are,*' they lectured, always and to all Áureas. '*Our motivation is everlasting. Alchemists do not live; we exist. Such a goal is not executed through a time-framed body, but achieved by sustaining a perennial attitude. Thus—*'

'*We have no boundaries, no frameworks of definitions, no rigid identities,*' less-human-Áurea finally answered, when all the others couldn't grasp the idea. *'That attitude carries us through an interminable existence, shaping our view of the universe.'*

Long ago, back in the obsidian room, she chuckled while pitying the human remains beneath the glass floor. "Élan," she lingered, frowning at the mentor. "Wouldn't existence be... by your words, a constant state across time, but... somehow volatile?"

Élan cawed, laughing and spreading their shadow wings. *'Existence is the most volatile state.'* they answered, tendrils spreading through matter to feed on the thunder, to bring forth the alive elements. *'Can't you comprehend, tot? To exist is to struggle, to war, to skirmish against the fluid alive element of identity! Over and over again, every event around you, every being you meet, every word you hear, every concept you learn... they change you! They alter your attitude until identity tumbles from one iteration to the other!'* The thoughts scattered through the Empty Room as the alchemist's voice rumbled. "You must find the core of what defines you, and use that to be true to yourself!"

Somewhen, somewhere, drowning in the Empty Room, less-human-Áurea stood up, scowling. Awareness sparkled in her, but comprehension shattered her.

"Find yourself! Weave the alive elements to compose your new self!" Élan shouted as they splintered the mentee.

Less-human-Áurea creaked, shredded, and puny shards of her identity spread into the Empty Room. Thoughts, emotions, memories, mental states, and even her body—they all succumbed to Élan's overpowering will.

The alchemist picked the pieces apart until Áurea's body flaked into stripes of flesh, threads of feathers, and strands of hair that evaporated into a crimson dust. Then, they turned to the mass of alive elements that had formed the mentee and flung them apart.

Her thought patterns were motes, dark and complex, and woven from words. Her emotions were colours and scents, her memories were fragments of images, and her mental states were clusters of shapes. Élan worked, methodical, willing each iota to vanish, to die, to disappear.

Eventually, some specks screamed in desperation, lacerated into alive elements so irrelevant and transient that they ceased to be. Yet others remained, clustering together into the core that had always defined the mentee; the piece of her willing to struggle for existence.

Desire to exist, fear to cease; the key alive elements of every alchemist. Around them danced Áurea's dominant traits. Her never-quelled wrath. Her intelligence and analytical prowess. Her raging craving for revenge. Her lurking second-guessing. Her bias and prejudice. The remnants of her humanity.

Those elements clustered together, and Élan left that mass defined as no-longer-Áurea alone. It was latent, pulsing with cravings—but whatever happened now, it was up to the mentee and not the mentor.

Therefore, Élan used those lingering moments to reshape into their true alchemical body. Two braids of shadow tendrils became legs armoured with penumbra. A mirage of nightmares and electricity formed metal-made faulds and a breastplate, gloom as night and foreboding as eternity. Shadow and darkness spread into four wings, each feather blending obsidian and steel. Black hair framed silver eyes, as their slender face displayed Élan's signature smirk.

The mass of no-longer-Áurea mumbled at that moment, recalling the mentor's attention. They watched it contort, splitting and merging, pulsing and growing until *five* clusters of existence appeared before it—and Élan's shock almost froze the Empty Room.

It was impossible, unfathomable. Unexpected and unforeseeable.

For once in their twenty millennia, Élan glimpsed a shard of The Rector's plans and of no-longer-Áurea's usefulness—and the revelation unlocked comprehension.

Those clusters were an alchemist's future possibilities, a prescription of the transfigurations they could achieve, always appearing like distant silhouettes during the first change—

except The Orders only had *four* types of alchemists, and only The Rector had somehow acquired them all.

Élan's shock evanesced, chased away by the pure delight that only the pursuit of knowledge could bring. Now, a fifth transfiguration was possible, fathomable. They were witnessing it—and within The Towers no less. Therefore, it was and would be achievable. This fifth, this new transfiguration, promised the evolution of The Orders. It challenged the status quo.

Somewhen, perchance, along the continuance of existence.

But at that moment, that prospect was quiescent. Dormant. Distant. The epitome of the struggle to exist. No-longer-Áurea could become a Soul Transmuter, but also something else; something so far unknown.

Suspended within the Empty Room, all five transfigurations yearned to be and longed to act—but most lacked the basis to do so now. The mentee had trained on a single type of elements, and for only one transfiguration.

Yet in that iota of time, that tot, that amorphous mass of alive elements so full of possibility crept towards one of the five silhouettes. The movement startled Élan, and their wings rippled with the euphoria of witnessing the genesis of change.

It shrieked, then. The mass of alive elements composing no-longer-Áurea. Vertiginous, vindictive, vivified. It expanded, like a veneer of contention, like a vicarious urge to discipline the vestiges and truths comprising the new identity. It consumed the space, it chased the figures, it reverberated with misery, with revulsion, with the exhilaration of ravaging and reshaping into someone beyond comprehension, beyond humanity.

Her desire combusted. Her fear consumed.

A myriad of alive elements rained like shooting stars over no-longer-Áurea as they crafted one transfiguration—and the other four silhouettes disappeared into the ether, waiting for the next moment to appear. The elements coalesced, struggling, morphing and reshaping. From non-physicality to a physical body, from life to existence, from timelined to timeless a Chimera slowly transfigured themselves.

Marvelled, the mentor hastened towards the new Soul Transmuter, rounding on the crouching figure to take in every detail. Their humanoid body wore a sculpted tight armour of engraved silver. Rose-gold locks brimmed like wired metal, cascading freely to blend with the feathers protruding from both shoulders. Finally, a helmet covered their head, topped with more feathers, all consistently alive.

Noticing the movement, the mentee giggled, raising their head and opening the visor of their helmet by sheer will. Their skin was pale lilac, drained of colour, and six eyes opened to the universe—brown, silver, gold.

Only then, Élan finally spoke the dawning question, "What are you?"

The new alchemist looked up, sat on their heels. "I'm the façade holding my realities together. I am Mien."

The mentor nodded at that Creed, delighted and daring—but another thought lingered in them. One that shaped a new purpose, based on what Mien had just revealed.

Whatever that fifth transfiguration was, Élan would acquire it.

Verve

5076-5077 CE

The months, fleeting and tediously long, vanished amidst the passive surveillance of an unexplainable human. For two years of unrelenting research, Verve wove observation with theory and facts with ideas, but only confirmed their uncertainty.

One night, like many others, they slithered between the potted plants, tendrils of shadow glamoured to invisibility. Iúrdan was, as usual, sprawled on the lectus, his face hidden under the crook of his elbow, the other arm barely holding his slippery sheet.

"Death... n–natural..." He snored, drooling and licking his lips. "Death... s–struggle... natural..."

The alchemist rippled with frustration. Every single event they had witnessed, every emotion on his soul-link, every piece of evidence stored for future studies only supported an ambiguous truth—their surveillance had been both a success and a failure.

Success, because Verve had proven their theory of shrouded alive elements that existed at different intensities by witnessing Iúrdan in a myriad of states across that spectrum. Failure, because they had found no reason behind those states, no supporting theory, no clues of how it intensified. That dichotomy baffled the alchemist.

During that time, Verve had added fragments of evidence

into their network, but the additions were disconnected—the pieces did not seem to relate. Once, Iúrdan's mind had thinly shrouded while dealing with mental ailments, but also while alone in the greenhouse after weeks of safe cases. One amputation had pushed the healer to a slightly deeper numbness, but another had barely registered on his memory. The strongest shroud had been incomparable to Peiro's and appeared when dealing with an allergic elder... while a child mauled by a wolf had only elicited a cold, methodical logic. Sporadically, Iúrdan's soul-link had fragmented when traversing the market and talking to some merchants, but the cases were bewildering and inconsistent. It had happened first when purchasing fruit, then when acquiring blades, and last when assessing garments.

Vexed, Verve slithered towards the sleeping healer, lifting a breeze; it carried the million scents blending within the greenhouse. Iúrdan stirred, pulling his pillow closer before sniffing and growling an inarticulate approximation of his characteristic motto.

In retrospect, Verve knew that their investigation was only a failure. The shrouded alive element existed within a disconnected spectrum that was as irreproducible as un-researchable. To their redoubled annoyance, the only consistent event had been Iúrdan's scheduled visits to his greenhouse, and the obnoxious repetition of his motto.

"D–death... n–a... t–tural..." he mumbled again, saliva pooling beneath his cheek.

Annoyed, Verve halted their review to assess the never-ending soul-link, but the only thoughts they discerned in his dreamless sleep were irrelevant thoughts about specific herbs. After all, The Rector's decisions were purposeful and supported by the understanding only accessible to their timeless, frameless existence. Therefore, if Iúrdan's relationship with plants was important, Hellion—the Chimera-Warlord with an affinity to plants—would have been assigned to—

Iúrdan snored, shuffling over the lectus and clenching his sheet. After a few groans, he rolled to his side, and the soul-link flooded with the memories of a flower. Relief flared from him, coating the exhausted healer with a lulling comfort.

Ignoring the tedious display, the alchemist slid between the sparks, moving into the healer's favourite desk. They rumbled with a thousand questions, rattling the zephyr within the greenhouse and upsetting the clouds high above in the sky. Once there, they plucked the most recurrent question and shaped it into a small whirlwind.

It ululated softly, whistling words inaudible to the human, "What is the unexplainable?"

Verve twisted their smoke-made form, countering that question with an extravagant proposition—asking *what* was a flawed approach. The Rector had vaguely defined the unexplainable as ground-breaking knowledge... and knowledge was knowledge, alchemical regardless of its area.

Under that assumption, Verve reformulated their question, triggering the zephyr to whistle, *"Why* is it unexplainable?"

The healer groaned, shivering and curling under the sheet.

Quieting the wind, Verve ignored the human, weaving a new thesis. The *why* could be the reason for the shroud, which kept that alive element undetectable for millennia. After a few moments of consideration, they concocted a simple plan. To wait for a natural occurrence of the shroud and escalate it to plunge Iúrdan into the most extreme case of the gap to determine *why* the element was hidden.

Their plan was possibly reckless and destructive, yet potentially revolutionary—and Verve chuckled, decided. If the former were to happen, The Rector would likely interfere... *somehow.* But if the latter occurred, it could be the key to solve that riddle of a mission.

To Verve, the benefits certainly outweighed the risks.

On the eve of dawn, the sky was a deep shade of azure streaked in mulberry near the horizon. The smallest sun was a slice of silver barely above it, while the trees' black silhouettes framed the world. Those hues blended into the marble roads, staining them with a glow ignored by the merchants.

Iúrdan stood on the corner between the two central roads,

mouth agape and gaze lost on the skyline. He blinked slowly, but that magnificent display of alluring colours only elicited the vague jitters of wonder and stupefaction—and Verve restarted the soul-link twice, ensuring the connection was active.

Moments later, the healer tucked a loose strand of black hair behind an ear and resumed his walk while Verve trailed behind, invisible. He was purposeful, hurrying through corners and traversing curvy roads. The houses spaced out, the flowerbeds ended, and the forest grew poignantly closer. Once at the settlement's edge, Iúrdan halted at the blacksmith's shop; its chimneys were steadily sputtering smoke, doors spread open.

Hesitating, the healer squeezed his fabric bag and meandered through the barren frontal garden before crossing the open threshold. The alchemist slipped behind him, blending with the soot coating the interior. The workshop had no subdivisions and was a large, rectangular room with blades scattered on a rack on the right, surrounded by pieces of metal and an assortment of tools. A sizable cooling tank lined the leftmost wall, while two anvils took the centre space, each aligned with its own forge. Fire burst savagely while the humans in front held a piece of metal with large pliers.

To Verve, the workshop flared with half-alive elements—fire and smoke, water and gas, sparks and sound waves. Those combined with the alive elements of the blacksmiths—pride and dreams, fears and plans—creating an interesting blend common in smithies. Settling their curiosity, the alchemist soared like dark smoke, hovering invisibly near the ceiling.

At the entrance, Iúrdan reclined on a creaking stool with a sooty cushion, leaning over a tall desk. He gawked at the toolset spread open for his perusal—a delicate, expert assortment of steel scalpels, scythes, and knives. A tall and muscular woman stood near the desk, dry lips cracking whenever she smiled at the healer. Her greying hair was buzzed short, and she wore a brown shirt and chausses hidden behind a worn leather apron.

"A magnificent set, Milia," Iúrdan whispered, studying the blades. "How much—?"

"Noth'eng," she replied, her chuckle as dark as her voice. "You 'eal mah people w'en we needed it. This is just gratitude."

He frowned, pointing at the tools, but she playfully deviated the conversation to other topics. To Verve, their banter oscillated between her inexhaustible gratitude for events Iúrdan considered minor, and his limitless admiration for the artisanship she deemed average. A boring combination the alchemist barely tolerated.

Suddenly, the forge roared to life, popping and hissing while the blacksmiths shouted, annoyed.

"Watch out!" Milia growled, turning towards the forges. She barely moved from the desk, pointing accusatory to the youngest, "Thet's enough, Saustín, pull it out!" She jutted her chin at the white-haired man beside him. "Watch 'im! 'e doesn't werk alone!"

White-hair nodded, grimacing with the ages-old exhaustion of having to supervise an unruly youngster, and Saustín flushed, tightening his grip on the pliers to hammer the molten metal. He was young, with black hair tied in a low tail and a remarkable likeness to Milia; she kept barking at the smithies, furious.

At first, Verve watched the humans near the forge, but then noticed Iúrdan as he slid from his stool, frowning.

In his first heartbeat, the healer bit his lower lips, pale green eyes etched on the forges, mind engrossed by the fire; the shroud rapidly took over his soul-link, veiling his alive elements. In the second, it flared with polychromatic embers, bright like relief, and scintillating like comfort. They sizzled around him, the only clear emotion within that veiled connection, but fading before his third heartbeat.

In the fourth heartbeat, Verve recognised those embers—and the shocking realisation dissipated their glamour. They stilled near the ceiling, fixed on the healer's soul-link.

Those sparks had appeared before, flaring within Iúrdan's soul-link whenever he was in the greenhouse. When he worked on the plants that brought him comfort, and while inspecting the flowerbeds that numbed his mind. When he pruned bushes and weeded out pots, and while mulling herbs and preparing concoctions.

In the fifth, Verve realised a truth that—due to lacking evidence—they hadn't yet considered. Those sparks were somehow related to the shroud or to the alive elements beneath; even when they had never appeared together before.

In the sixth heartbeat, desire thundered within the alchemist. A craving so profound, so abyssal and unfathomable, it redefined the concept of infinity. It vanished all risks, all considerations, all deliberations. It overpowered Verve's senses, ravaging their plans and reforging them anew with a single-minded, tripartite reason.

To learn. To know. To comprehend.

In the seventh heartbeat, Verve soul-linked Saustín, soul-shaping his mind until his hearing quieted, and the sounds died before his ears, meaningless. The alchemist flooded him with courage and anger, and the rascal youngster thrust the hammered metal into the forge, leaning closer despite Milia's loud objections. Verve insisted, forcing Saustín to disregard the heat, the blazing metal, and the surrounding sparks.

In the eighth heartbeat, Verve froze Saustín in place while Milia shouted and the other blacksmiths ignored the row. Altering the air near the forge, the alchemist fed the fire and forced it to consume everything in their wake. It reignited, exploding out of the hearth—cobalt on the base, tongues soaring orangey, metal sparks riding the crest, bursting from the edges.

White-hair howled, pulled back by his panic and experience, back turned towards the fire, head covered beneath his aged hands—but Saustín remained locked. He smiled, right eyelid melting by the heat, hand clasping the pliers while the flames consumed half his body, eating his clothes and long hair.

For three more heartbeats, Verve held Saustín's soul-shaped and frozen until Milia screamed. After another, and the alchemist released their hold when two blasts of warm water slammed against Saustín. Two other volleys smothered him, and after a transient silence, the workshop shattered under the howls of a maimed youngster and the shrieks of his terrified mother.

In truth, Saustín didn't matter; none of them did. To Verve, those humans were a means to a goal: tools and nothing else.

Experiments, short-lived and doomed to a brief existence subjugated to their alive elements.

But Iúrdan *mattered*. He was the sole purpose of Verve's mission, the cause of all their actions, the problem and the solution—and, unknowingly, he captured the alchemist's attention. Once again, his soul-link was so thoroughly veiled that Verve only perceived an abyss filled by the undetectable, but now illuminated by the sparks. Those innocent, relieving and incoherent polychromatic shards that Verve had once labelled as relief and comfort.

Amidst that unexplainable mind-state, Iúrdan stomped forwards, functional and coherent. He grabbed an apprentice and demanded a cart, visually inspecting white-hair before kneeling near Saustín and tearing apart the remnants of his clothes. Through that process, Verve only captured the shattered and incongruous ideas wailing from the healer's mind, intertwining with his controlled, commanding voice.

Orders, whole and audible. To restrain Milia, to hurry with the cart, to bring a clean sheet. Thoughts, fragmented and incomplete. Infection, pain, fire, struggle, internal, airways, damage, reckless, unstoppable, death, natural, breathing, pulse. Orders, assertive and specific. To move Saustín, to carry him gently, to raise his chest and right arm, to cover him, to hurry to his clinic.

Horses neighed, rearing under the whip, and the cart rolled through the marble roads. Milia screeched in the distance, fighting someone—but her terror faded, unimportant to the healer. The redhead driver whipped the animals, cursing under her breath until they accelerated, turning on the corners as the cart's wood shrieked in tandem. Iúrdan knelt beside the youngster, hissing commands to white-hair—who held Saustín and his sheet with trembling, burnt hands.

Verve chased them, hooked into that soul-link and riding the dawn's cool breeze. They were traversing the market with a patient whose right arm and half of his face had melted—yet the healer's mind was unreadable to the alchemist. Shrouded so thickly it seemed deserted of all alive elements sans the fragmented shards of incongruous thought patterns focused on Saustín's survival.

It was, without a doubt, the most riveting experiment so far.

Iúrdan remained calm as the cart drifted to a stop in front of his house, and white-hair lifted the boy. Verve loomed over as he directed the older blacksmith to move the boy, coherent yet living in the most unorthodox mind state the alchemist had ever witnessed.

Never in their twenty thousand years had Verve seen a mind so unreadable, so cryptic and illegible when soul-linked. The juxtaposition was impossible, and the alchemist observed, ambitious like a researcher on the eve of a ground-breaking discovery.

Once in the patients' room, white-hair wailed and collapsed on a stool, his sobs louder than Saustín's bellows. Meanwhile, the redhead driver whispered to him, restraining her tears and frowning at Iúrdan. He dashed into the inner corridors, snatching a basket and filling it with bottles, herbs pouches, the portable heater, and a leather roll with tools. Verve trailed behind, documenting the process on their network of evidence before returning to the room alongside the healer.

Iúrdan frowned at the patient, lips pursed into a line—but remained in his mindless state, acting with precision and moving like a strategist. Disciplined and orderly, carrying action after action so mechanical and factual that Verve only perceived the sequence of actions.

He turned the heater and warmed a vinegar bottle, force-feeding leaves to Saustín. He relaxed, mumbling unintelligibly while the healer cut and discarded his charred clothes. When done, Iúrdan checked his breathing, demanded the boy to be held, grabbed the heated bottle with a tool, and spread warm vinegar over the burns. The dazed, intoxicated patient moaned but Iúrdan ignored him, retrieving two large rolls of gauze from a cupboard and the jars of royal jelly from the basket. Leaning closer, he sunk the clean straps in it and covered the wounds starting on the head and crossing the melted eyelids. Then, he protected the cheeks and necks, bandaging the charred, brownish right shoulder and arm.

In that rational stillness, Verve witnessed the long and time-consuming process while thoroughly aware of the surrounding chaos. A mayhem of alive elements flashed painfully from white-hair as he sat in that corner, hands on his forehead, tears in his eyes. A hailstorm of fear sputtered from the redhead as she helped the healer. A cyclone of destruction rolled through the waiting room, while Milia kicked chairs and screamed in uncontrollable terror, fighting someone until he knocked her out. A commotion of curious onlookers boiled outside, gossiping so loudly that Verve noticed the voices, perceived their emotions, and heard the echoes of their thoughts.

Yet Iúrdan was impervious.

To the Chimera-Warlord, his mind was shrouded. Impenetrable yet flooding the soul-link with alive elements that Verve vaguely perceived—and for once in their interminable existence, they could sense the bare shape of things, but never its nuances. The only difference they noticed was those seemingly misplaced embers of relief, which now swirled around Iúrdan like a crown, falling like feathers on the wind only to soar again.

Iúrdan procedure was lengthy, and when he placed the last gauze, hands dripping honey-scented jelly, the chaos had subsided—or perhaps Verve didn't notice it, enthralled by the healer's mind. He sighed, nodding to the redhead and leaning to time his breathing. Its rhythm reverberated within the soul-link for a few heartbeats until Iúrdan nodded, wiping his hands on a remnant of gauze while scowling at the portable heater.

In a heartbeat—one after so many others, so similar yet so different—his mind was deeply veiled to the alchemist. It only revealed the intuitive acknowledgement of his need to turn off the heater.

In the next heartbeat—one that Verve would never forget—Iúrdan's sparks blasted from his mind, exploding like colourful fireworks while his eyes etched on that dying flame. Those ideas were continuous, unrestrained, whizzing while soaring and scattering in luminous flares, motes flickering with unseen shapes, speckles colouring in unknown hues. They subsisted, jaded and sated, as the healer leaned against the wall and slid, mindless, onto the floor.

Verve remained in that room for hours, like a stunned coil of silver smoke, invisible and lost in thought.

Verve, who had caused the rise and fall of a thousand civilisations. Verve, a prodigious Soul Transmuter and a deft Protean Reshaper. Verve, the first and sole witness of the unexplainable, of the incomprehensible.

Mid morning, with a clear sky and a soft breeze. A crowd of onlookers gathered outside Iúrdan's clinic, gossiping, restless, not daring to enter the chaotic waiting room. A blacksmith carried Milia, dropped her on a horse, rode out towards her house. Verve stood on the rooftop, their humanoid smoke-form invisible to prying eyes, mind shocked by a hundred ideas not yet considered.

It had been so long since they had not comprehended something, since they had committed so many mistakes.

Noon, with a crisp cerulean sky, and brightly lit roads. The market's noises flared in the distance, scents blending in the natural breeze. A cart parked outside the clinic, and white-hair carried Saustín out—sedated and with half his body bandaged. Verve remained on the rooftop.

A question circled them, dancing on the wind: why hadn't they realised the embers of relief were part of the shroud? Then: what if they'd appeared before?

The alchemist watched the wind, locked in the questions they couldn't solve. Not yet, at least.

Why had they missed this? Why did the shroud exist? Why did they perceive it but not understand it? Why, why, why?

Afternoon, with dimmer light, colder breeze, and an empty clinic. Iúrdan lay on his lectus on the greenhouse, body covered by his worn-out sheet, mind entirely shrouded. Alighting onto the glass rooftop, Verve glanced askance at the unreadable man, three certainties framing their actions.

For five years, they had observed only half of the unexplainable, crafting useless experiments that slanted their observations to fit a flawed theory. For five years, they had disregarded meaningful information. For five years, they had asked the wrong questions without realising it.

It was exasperating, infuriating; the awareness of having committed so many errors. It was exciting, electrifying; the possibility of learning from those failures.

"Struggle is natural..." Iúrdan whispered inside the greenhouse, shaky. "I eased his pain, gave him a chance..."

The Chimera-Warlord looked down, eyes narrowing to carmine slits. Iúrdan was calm except for his trembling voice, and the embers of relief flickered around him, evidencing another of Verve's mistakes—they had misclassified that emotion and disregarded it entirely. Those embers were not relief, but shards of an alive element Verve still failed to identify. Exactly as with the shrouded ones, the shards were visible but unreadable.

Dusk, staining the sky cobalt and aubergine, clouds arriving from the south. The healer slept, restless and exhausted, his soul-link dreamless and peaceful. Verve groaned, seeing the connection and focusing on the only detail they had correctly theorised about.

Iúrdan produced alive elements within a spectrum of intensities, but shrouded and incomprehensible to Verve. The reason remained unknown, the elements were unknown, and its cause was—frustratingly—also unknown.

Night, clear and cold, with a rim of silver in the horizon, a sky of twinkling stars, a splotch of an amethyst galaxy traversing the zenith. Beneath it, Verve brew a new question. Could *they* be the cause of the shroud?

They blinked, gaze wandering from the stirring human to the plants, the town at night, and the sky above—and, finally, Verve *understood*.

The cause of the shroud, its relationship with the shards, the reason for Verve's own blindness, the origin of the unexplainable and what it was. All the questions, all the incongruities, all the errors were easily explained by two notions intrinsic to Verve, to existence itself.

Bias and boundaries. The cage limiting comprehension, stalling progress.

Verve *laughed*, loud and unrestrained, stalling the breeze and muting the sounds. The answers were obvious, but they had been too biased to understand, too bounded by their knowledge to accept the evidence.

Biased, because Verve had been an alchemist for so long that alchemy prejudiced them to interpret the world only according to what they comprehended. That bias blinded them to anything *beyond* the known alchemical rules—and it was their worst enemy; subconscious, contrary to beliefs, and rapid to discard and destroy evidence against it. It was perennial and unbeatable unless accepted and surveyed in aeternum. Regardless of their endless existence, even alchemists comprehended the world according to their knowledge and experience—and Verve was guilty of it. Through this mission, they had biased reality by searching for evidence that supported only the known, only the comfortable, only the peer-accepted view of the universe upon which current alchemy was construed.

Bounded, because the base for alchemy was will and knowledge, and Verve had been chasing its nemesis. A thought so absurd that only a human, not shackled to alchemical rules, could think of it. A piece of knowledge so far removed from current alchemical boundaries that it had to be accepted as a truth without proof. An idea so impractical and inconceivable that it was unexplainable with the current knowledge. A contradiction.

Biased, because since arriving, Verve had focused only on

the clues that confirmed their supposition—that Iúrdan was ordinary, that his closeness to death and suffering had numbed him. They had never observed without judging, instead crafting experiments to confirm their incorrect presumptions.

Bounded, because their observations thereafter had been incomplete; studied with the current rules of alchemical knowledge. Verve had repeatedly seen only what they understood, misinterpreting clues, mislabelling emotions, and likely committing other mistakes.

Biased, because they had discarded the shards simply because the phenomenon appeared only when Iúrdan worked on the plants—a half-alive element that was *not* Verve's speciality. This prejudice had led the alchemist to disregard whether those shards related only to plants or to all half-alive elements.

Bounded, because they had related the shards to the shroud only when they sparked near the fire—a half-alive element closer to their affinity. After all, unlike Soul Transmuters, Proteans' affinity to a few half-alive limited the complexity of their alchemy... and this boundary had affected Verve's perception.

Bias and boundaries, because Verve had never wondered what thoughts Iúrdan's shroud hid. The alchemist had maimed the evidence, assuming that those thoughts were about other alive elements, such as the mental states or emotions related to his patients... which was sensible, reasonable even, given Iúrdan's profession as a healer. However, the shards, those pesky embers, had appeared when Iúrdan directly interacted with half-alive elements—plants, fire, and so many others.

Bias and boundaries, because they had steered Verve away from a question that was now unavoidable. Could Iúrdan's shrouded alive elements be thoughts about half-alive elements?

Verve stalled, slowly glancing at the surrounding ones—the air and its moisture, the clouds and its charges, the sound waves and its echoes. The plants and spores on Iúrdan's greenhouse and in the town's gardens. The lanterns fire across the road.

So many new hypotheses to test, so many clues likely ignored. So much knowledge lost to that inherent, unbeatable prejudice. So much more to gain now that it was evident.

Shocked, Verve glanced at the sleeping human and snapped their fingers. The motion recreated The Rector's voice, as it repeated a clue that only now made sense.

"He is a key," The Rector's voice hissed, swirling around Verve and echoing repetitiously. "He is a key. A key. A key."

So convoluted but so straightforward. The healer was a key to unlock Verve's understanding of their own bias—but also to reveal knowledge beyond current alchemical boundaries.

Verve needed to probe Iúrdan again.

The Chimera-Warlord worked with purpose. They spent two mornings carefully planning, eagerly awaiting the Autumn Market, and ignoring the onslaught of patients arriving at the clinic. Then, they invested those afternoons and nights to prepare the experiment. It had to seem natural to the humans; nothing else than the weather's unpredictability.

Therefore, Verve assembled the clouds near Acero Gulf, blew the wind north-west, and hurried the brewing storm across Carbona. The journey recharged the cumulus, darkening them into masses of charcoal and iron, rolling through the sky and into the fringe town housing Iúrdan's clinic.

On the third morning, the alchemist glided invisibly among the looming currents. From above, they saw the central roads lined with the market stalls, and crammed with meandering onlookers. The inns and taverns brimmed with tourists and locals, and their merriment cluttered the space, muting down the distant groans of the fast approaching clouds; a thick ribbon of iron devouring the cerulean zenith from the south. But as expected, everyone remained fixed on their tasks, ignoring the world—just like Iúrdan. He was checking fruits, smelling their scent and oblivious to the impending doom.

As the clouds approached, Verve circled the plaza, lightning slithering in their wake. The sky darkened, the clouds roared, and the wind hastened into a strong breeze. Most humans noticed the ever-darkening horizon, but some simply secured their stalls with stones, while others covered their products or donned their hoods.

In that moment, high above and hidden from them, Verve transmuted into their true alchemical body. A humanoid figure, with a tight and seamless armour of iridescent, gold-white metal. Ringlets of soot-made hair trailed from underneath their brocas helmet, while smoke seeped from beneath the pauldrons, meshing into an interminable cloak. Amethyst sparks blasted from Verve's back, and tendrils of lightning shaped their wings, framing metal-made feathers.

Spreading those surreal wings, the Chimera-Warlord soared around the market, taking on the crowd. They found Iúrdan near a stall, arranging vegetables into his cloth bag. He glanced up, and Verve soul-linked him just when a vague memory of the greenhouse flared through the connection, sparking the shattered embers once mislabelled as relief. The connection was shrouded, illuminated by the shards.

The storm groaned on Verve's command, eclipsing the noon and whistling with an irreverent gale—and sudden mayhem cluttered the road. Merchants stashed goods and disassembled stalls; adults hurried toddlers and elders to safety while horses neighed, shaking carts and adding to the chaos.

Focused on their target, Verve wriggled lightning from their wings, willing the clouds to recharge. The sky flashed azure and mauve amidst the gunmetal sky, eliciting shouts from the crowd assembled on the market road. Verve hadn't soul-linked the townspeople, but their natural perception flooded with a myriad of alive elements—trepidation, restlessness, urgency, consternation, worry, distress. They ignored those emotions, isolating Iúrdan's soul-link and focusing on his shroud. He was assisting a merchant, locking her crates of vegetables with the same logical calmness that guided his hands during surgeries.

His sparks were fading, and Verve acted quickly, altering the temperature, adding pressure, and raining small hail onto the marble roads. Granules first, sporadic and erratic, pin-sized but sturdy enough to tip-tap rhythmically over a hundred surfaces. Small pebbles right after, pattering on the crates, scaring animals and humans alike—but not Iúrdan, whose tranquillity was absolute. Amidst that nascent storm, his polychromatic shards continued to fade, verging on extinction.

Annoyance thundered within the alchemist, and they soared to will the air, the temperature, the wind—and the hailstorm grew, larger and brutal, cobbles drumming on the marble, on the animals, on the people. They growled and cursed out loud, bracing heads and running heedlessly, sliding on the slippery roads, stumbling onto others and searching for refuge.

Amidst that chaos, Verve inspected the crowd to focus on a woman down the road; she was pulling the reins of her donkeys, swearing and slipping over the wet floor. They pointed at her, willing a cobble-sized hail to smash onto her forehead; she moaned after the hit, tumbling back while the rock bounced, hitting the ground and cracking. Iúrdan saw the elder and the cobble, and his thoughts flared brightly, the shards reigniting polychromatic. He dashed across the road, catching the woman and inspecting her bloodied head—while his shroud thinned, losing opacity.

Verve cocked their head, ringlets of soot and smoke tumbling over their iridescent pauldrons, bewilderment narrowing the crimson eyes. The soul-link was brimming with alive elements, blurred and hazy under the fading veil, but noticeable enough to reveal how they wove into a net—but Verve's visibility was limited.

There was clarity, but there wasn't; there was something, but there wasn't.

While Iúrdan dragged the bleeding woman, Verve coerced another hail to shatter, and shards sparked from the healer. Enthused, the alchemist found another target to damage with hail. Then another, and another and another and another. They created a sequence, spurring the healer to action, and watching as each human mauled by the hail thinned Iúrdan's shroud. Each added details into the soul-link, revealing more elements and weaving more connections—but never enough for the alchemist to comprehend them.

In that abyssal noon, darkened by the merry music of destruction, Verve spread their arms, directing their orchestra of wind and lightning. It slithered through the sky, sneaking between the clouds, thundering ominously and silencing the wails and howls beneath. Ushered by the gale, the doors slammed in their frames, animals ran heedlessly, and pieces of the stalls rolled through the streets. The lightning flared, threatening, deafening, moving with the precision innate to the alchemist made of thoughts and thunder.

Iúrdan rushed to hide while Verve tracked him, intrigued by that soul-link so clear yet so unclear. Eventually, he reached a deep balcony, and sheltered beneath it. His eyes narrowed as he focused on the incessant downpour, trailing the brilliant snakes of thunder that reflected on the pools of water. Each flash brightened his soul-link, revealing more sparks and thinning the remnants of the shroud—but not enough; *never* enough.

Enthralled and intrigued, yet precise and methodical, Verve selected a new target and willed the lightning to slither between the nearest clouds, repositioning the electricity. Iúrdan's veil was translucent when he scowled at the clouds growling above the town's central tree. Taller than any building, it was surrounded by a large marble roundabout now clogged with abandoned carts, and harbouring a dozen shivering humans.

The healer gaped when his gaze met theirs, and the soul-link normalised as Verve felt his ominous fear fade while wrestling with hope—to remain safe, to remain unharmed. Eager, the alchemist willed his lightning to attack that emotion.

The clouds groaned, rumbling in anger until the thunder plunged. Once, like claws seeking its target. Twice, like terror opening its jaws to kill. Thrice, like a whip, thick and unrelenting, discharging into the largest tree.

The sheltering humans howled, but it was nothing more than open mouths and widened eyes, wails deafened by the thunder-strike. The trunk blasted with fire, sliced by the lightning, bursting in flames while electricity surged into a cloud of white light and burnt leaves. Splinters rained over the people beneath it while the halved trunk collapsed, unable to sustain the branches' weight. They tore apart when the lightning retreated, plunging and crushing the humans that hadn't escaped yet. The crown followed in quarters, pieces plummeting aflame, creaking while the humans beneath shrieked.

The thunder roared, the sound waves sluggish compared to the light, but deafening the world. Iúrdan froze, gaze etched in the burning tree. Intrigued, Verve perused his alive elements with increasing eagerness—the shroud had faded, and the soul-link now brimmed with thoughts, beliefs, and feelings, shaped like threads weaving together, forming a net, splitting into paths and braiding mental states. The shards were part of it, glitter shimmering within his mind, like ideas or feelings attached to the thoughts.

Yet amidst that everlasting moment, and after inspecting those alive elements, the alchemist comprehended nothing.

It was analogous to abstract art, lying in front of someone's eyes but puzzling and cryptic. It was like hearing another language, noticing the sounds and details but unable to interpret them. It was akin to scanning an unknown script, observing the symbols but lacking their meaning.

For a moment, the downpour hammered the flooded roads, spluttering in the pooling water, constant and irrevocable. In the next moment, the Chimera-Warlord quelled the wind, softened the rain into a miserable drizzle, and left the clouds to impede the sky.

Verve didn't need to continue the experiment. They had learned all they could. Their awareness of their own bias had shredded the shroud, but their alchemical boundaries were unbreachable.

Iúrdan's elements were explicit, and his shards now shone with their correct shape—but to the alchemist, that whole was unexplainable. Its secrets could not be learned by mere observation. After all, any meaningful acquisition of logical knowledge required understanding the significance of what was witnessed; a feat unachievable without a teacher.

One willing to impart his wisdom, or coerced to do so.

Élan

5077 CE

Élan's footfalls crackled with unspent electricity, shadowy tendrils rippling in its wake. Anxious but not desperate, although their cadence announced their intention to The Towers—to find The Rector, to speak to them. Thus, the corridors twisted and bent, repositioning staircases and aligning dimensions until the alchemist found a specific double-sheeted door. It was crafted in obsidian marble that slid open to reveal an inky darkness.

After crossing the threshold, Élan landed in the Mirrors Room—an infinite corridor where every surface was a speculum. They peered at the reflections, where the mirror split their *current* self into their completed transfigurations; those that Élan had seen during their first change and subsequently achieved. A Soul Transmuter farther left, a Matter Transmuter closer by. Potential forms should have appeared as well, mostly as hazy silhouettes... but there was none nearby. Nothing else was available to them.

The raven-alchemist chuckled sourly at the lack, their armour rippling with electricity. Never in their twenty millennia had they wished to comprehend The Rector's plans, instead accepting them as a truth that already was. But that had changed the instant when, through Mien's evolution, Élan had glimpsed a possibility that could change The Orders—a fifth transfiguration.

They craved it, unreasonably so. Even if the mirrors didn't reflect it.

"Yet that won't stop you," The Rector's voice echoed further down the corridor.

The commanding alchemist hovered between the mirrors in the distance, gaze etched in Élan. The four swords floating around them spun like a compass of glyphs, unperturbed as they glanced at the newcomer.

Not ashamed of their desires, Élan bowed while peeking askance at their leader's reflections. Three clear shapes stood tall on the left—Soul and Matter Transmuters, and the Protean Reshaper. Meanwhile, their right only reflected a Machina Reshaper—yet the instant Élan noticed the hazy, fifth figure blurred beside it, the Mirrors Room was no longer.

Suddenly, both alchemists stood amidst an abyssal blackness at paces from each other.

Élan took a knee, both gauntleted hands grazing the floor, wings folded back like a hazy cloak of feathery shadows. Whatever happened now, even that visit, was undoubtedly within The Rector's plans—as it always was.

"All hail Élan, the mightiest Full Transmuter, the chaos-tamer, the record-breaker. The first alchemist to transfigure a mentee in five human years," The Rector chuckled, facing the other. "And the first one, besides myself, to witness the *fifth*."

Élan looked up to the commanding alchemist, but their gaze soon diverted towards The Rector's scimitar. It hovered around, pointing to the mirror that had reflected the Machina Reshaper transfiguration. It was an instant, a minor clue, but it opened a dam of information Élan had long overseen as trivia.

The myths surrounding The Rector's impossible journey through the four alchemical transfigurations. The certainty that they had added the Machina last. The shared understanding that Machinas couldn't be combined with any other transfiguration. That every alchemical transfiguration, except Machinas, always reflected on the viewers' left. The theories long forgotten. The Rector's command before assigning Áurea—now Mien

—to Élan's care. The hazy reflection on The Rector's right. Élan's craving for knowledge, and their reasons to seek their leader.

"You are chasing the correct clues, raven one. I expected nothing else from the most powerful of the ten Full Transmuters," The Rector teased in a challenging whisper. They rolled their gauntleted fingers, commanding. "Stand and speak. Freely... for *now*."

Élan jolted to their feet, electricity sparkling from their half-spread wings. Eagerness swarmed their voice as they rushed, "Mien's fifth possibility is a new alchemical transfiguration, and you knew it. You have been searching for it. I want it; I'll do anything for it."

"You don't know what you crave..." The Rector warned, certain but never threatening.

"Then teach me," Élan rebuked, resolved.

Courage and dauntlessness swirled within them, and Élan transmuted their own emotions into a non-fear state. Once calmed, they met The Rector's infinite eyes—three of them, each a window into written and unwritten knowledge, shadowed by their obsidian cowl.

"Before I can do so, you must pay the price, Élan. *Reason*. Use those clues," The Rector's whisper died as they grinned. It was the challenging snarl of someone directing the bleeding edge of the razor cutting through the veil forbidding new knowledge.

Slowly, The Rector lifted a hand, palm up, summoning three glyphs. Each encased in a crystalline sphere composed of the alchemical element it represented—non-alive, half-alive, and alive. On cue, their scimitar glided towards the left-most wall, piercing the darkness and revealing the three figures of a Soul Transmuter, a Matter, and a Protean Reshaper.

Élan assessed them with the greedy look of a student striving for comprehension, gaze darting between the shapes and the elemental spheres. It was a clue; they were certain. That triad was the foundation of The Orders' comprehension of existence—except that the fifth transfiguration now indicated a gap in the knowledge.

But what was that missing knowledge? What could that transfiguration do?

Challenged, Élan fixed on the glyphs, and lore-weaved themselves to review their own past knowledge without expenditure of time.

Amidst the depths of the lore-weaving, the alchemist saw the stages of their own knowledge. First, not-Élan; the dark-haired human male who, twenty millennia ago, had transfigured into half-Élan. A Soul Transmuter, and the first step of their alchemical journey. Young-Élan, was also there; the Full Transmuter just after their second transfiguration, but vastly different from their current state.

Among the four of them, knowledge flowed freely. Memories resurfaced as not-Élan recalled his time in the Library—he had once asked the same questions every candidate wondered and every alchemist denied. The same enquiries Élan pondered now.

Why were there only three elements? Why was the Protean called Reshaper if it *created* elements? Why did Proteans reflect with the Transmuters? Why did Machinas prevent any other transfiguration? Why Matter-Proteans couldn't combine elements like Machinas did? Why were non-alive and alive elements non-combinable? How had The Rector transfigured into a Machina? How could Élan evolve?

For what seemed an eternity, Élan and not-Élan mouthed those questions in turns until half-Élan waved them away. To that iteration of the alchemist, the answers were *evident*. The three elements were unchallengeable; nothing disproved them. Likewise, The Orders were four, and only four, because many alchemists had searched for others only to vanish after crossing thresholds of unavailable knowledge.

"Proteans are Reshapers for their affinity to half-alive elements," half-Élan stated once, when training their first mentee.

Within the lore-weaving, Élan, the latest iteration, the daring one, the mentor of the impossible, grimaced. Those were facts, all facts. All supported by evidence, yet all dubious.

That seed of uncertainty brought another memory; when young-Élan had silenced another mentee.

"I told you already," the Raven One had said, and their voice echoed back through the lore-weaving. "Through millennia, The Orders have researched. Everything has been tested and discarded, over and over, as enabled by The Towers. We have confirmed this; The Orders' knowledge of the elements is complete."

Displeased, Élan brushed those recollections away from the lore-weaving, focusing on another. Not-Élan stood again in the Library, standing with arms spread open, a network of books connected into his clumsy mind-stretch. The old and shabby one at the centre was the base for a network of theories and hypotheses that expanded through time.

Among that network, lay comprehension. Beyond it, lay evolution.

"No theory will hold on to current times, regardless of how long it has sustained," Élan whispered, interrupting the lore-weaving.

The Full Transmuter met The Rector's gaze. Barely a split second had passed, but it had been enough. They had pieced together the questions from their youth, the evidence witnessed during Mien's transfiguration, and the reflections at The Rector's left.

"For aeons, alchemists misunderstood Proteans," Élan stated, beckoning to the corresponding glyph. "Currently, The Orders argue that Proteans and Machina are Reshapers because of their affinity for half-alive elements, historically considered *less than* the other two elements... except they are all equally funda-mental to alchemy." They spread a wing, pointing at the trio of reflections on The Rector's left. "Long ago, I asked the same questions I ask now. Proteans coerce and create half-alive elements through their will, which in principle, is what Soul or

Matter Transmuters do with either alive or non-alive elements, respectively."

The Rector nodded, and when they raised a hand, the dark haze evaporated. Both alchemists stood again in the Mirrors Room, the width of the corridor somehow accommodating them. The four reflections—and the hazy silhouette—surrounding The Rector cocked their heads, watching the transgressing Full Transmuter.

"Go on, keep explaining," they commanded, irrefutable.

The raven-alchemist grinned, starving for knowledge but eager like a pupil who'd just figured out an impossible riddle.

"Proteans were once posed as Transmuters simply because the Mirrors Room always reflects them on the left." Their cadence accelerated the more they explained. "There are three elements, hence, there are three phases of transmutation... but The Orders let prejudice stain our quest for knowledge." Élan's right wings flared to point at the rightmost reflections. "There are only three elements, and if we assume that non-alive and alive elements are truly non-combinable, hence, the fifth transfiguration is the true Reshaper we have been missing. One that bridges half-alive and alive elements to—"

"To create *sentience*. To animate. That transfiguration is the impossible henceforth possible! An Anima Reshaper!" The Rector rumbled, their voice splitting into four tones and a whisper.

They shook their palm, and the glyphs soared to orbit above their heads. The Rector's fingers twitched, their blades realigned around them, and five new glyphs materialised around the elements'. Three aligned above, representing the true Transmuters—Soul, Matter, Protean; the last two hung below and in between the elements' glyphs, suggesting the Reshapers—Machina and Anima. Two suitable counterparts, two halves set to reshape existence.

Abyssal darkness enveloped them again—yet Élan's silverish eyes etched on that fifth transfiguration. Craving it, coveting it, claiming it for themselves.

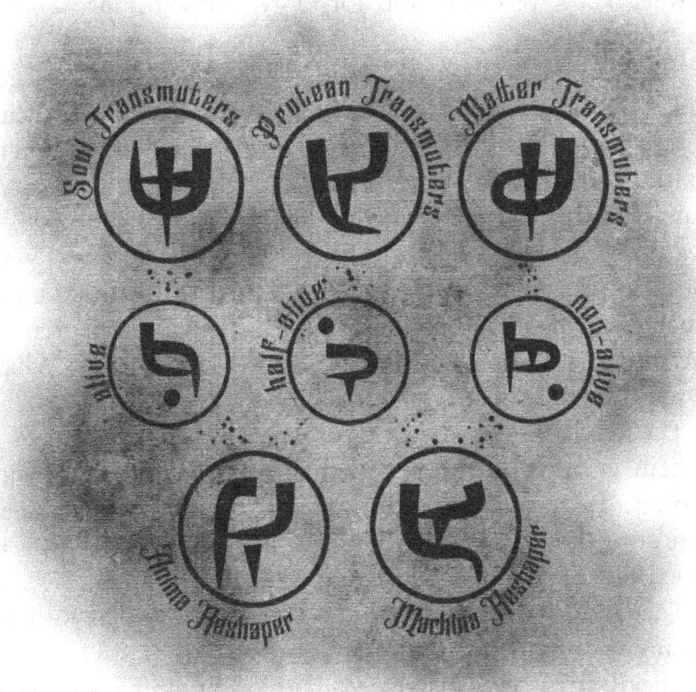

"It is exactly as you thought during the lore-weaving. No theory holds into current times, regardless of how long it has prevailed." The Rector's sibilant murmur censored that lust for knowledge. "Change may be daunting, and sameness may be comfortable, but one is the path to evolution, and the other is the cliff to stagnation and decay. Our systems, timeless as they are, are not immune to progression and maturation." The Rector lectured, unchallengeable, owning the truth as they beckoned to the glyphs.

Élan's shadows rattled, electricity sparkling within their nightmarish armour—a faithful representation of the inner chaos startling their thoughts.

Untamed knowledge lay open before both alchemists. Teasing and taunting, but skittish and slippery. Just like lightning replenished its electricity, knowledge fuelled Élan's existence. The pursuit of knowledge was their reason to be, to act, to wait. They were ravenous for more, for self-improvement, for evolution.

"This..." Élan whispered, eager. "This could change..." They choked, elated. "This will change *everything!*" They howled, exultant. "The Orders, the alchemists. Existence and all its dimensions! It will redefine and restructure alchemy!" Their roar thundered through the abyss, and their wings spread open. "I *need* that knowledge, Rector. The Machina Reshaper was your last quarter; the impossible feat that vested you with an unattainable and unequivocal authority. How did you do it? *How?* There must be something that enabled the impossible. Whatever you did, I will do. Tell me, tell me, *tell me!*"

The Reactor towered over Élan. "Why do you ask?"

Élan grinned, intoxicated with hypotheses, delirious with theories. "Because if you transfigured into the impossible, then replicating those steps could allow me to evolve. To add fifths to my existence and unlock my Anima Reshaper!"

That craving clamoured around them, startling The Rector's floating swords and winding Élan's wings.

The Rector's eyes narrowed, corners crinkling roguishly. "How indeed..." Echoes, again in their four voices and a whisper. "The truth is very simple, Élan. Knowledge cannot be shared unless it develops from intuition to systematic logic... otherwise, you would just distribute a dogma. This is why we force our mentees to experience the elements." They chuckled, and bits of ideas spread from them like iridescent specks. "Transfigurations are gradual, just like the discovery of knowledge. Like grains of sand piling atop each other, theories and theorems blend within a candidate's mind to shape a greater understanding. Yet regardless of this effort, some knowledge is *contradictory.*"

Élan frowned, confused for the first time in centuries. "Knowledge is never contradictory."

"Exactly!" The Rector smiled, their speech hastening with their eagerness to teach. "Someone's knowledge is, always, *incomplete...* and the missing parts, those gaps, make it *seem* contradictory! That is why Machinas cannot transfigure into anything else, Élan. Because the understanding required to combine elements contradicts the one needed to create them! We lack the bridge between them!" The Rector laughed, and the golden wings on their temples moved forward, framing the hushed whispering of a secret. "Once an alchemist comprehends existence to Transmute, Reshaping becomes impossible, and vice versa. For now, we can't bridge that gap; the bias acquired after learning is too mind-bending to allow anything else. Unless..." An enunciation, so soft it was almost soundless. "—unless the alchemist forcibly incorporates that knowledge into theirs."

That whisper slithered around the alchemists. The Rector licked their own lips in an animalistic representation of that thirst for knowledge that levelled all alchemists—and that gesture was all that Élan needed to comprehend.

"You *amalgamated* a Machina Reshaper..." They stuttered, at a loss for words. "—or many."

The Rector's blades swirled to point at the reflected silhouette of their Machina. "Not every alchemist transfigures to *be*, Élan. Some are only meant to *educate* others and enable further growth... whether within the Transmuters or the Reshapers. Perhaps only until we fill the gaps within our knowledge."

In a moment, nothing. In another, everything.

A thousand questions; uncountable, unwordable. Unreasonable for an alchemist like Élan, unthinkable to anyone else— where, what, why, what if, how come, who, when, how. Enquiries startled them, theories changed them, answers evolved them.

The alive elements forming half of Élan mutated within them, morphing into a new self with a new understanding. Those elements were so excruciatingly comprehensive that they burst out of the alchemist like colourful motes, materialising thought patterns that collided in the surrounding space. They were alive—oh so alive—and they birthed stars. Miniature suns of theories and hypotheses. Wormholes of questions and answers. Galaxies of proofs and logic. They shone gold and blue, red and white, swarming in seas of polychromatic nebulas.

Amidst that mayhem, The Rector refocused Élan, pinching their chin with a hand.

"I'll share two more secrets with you," The Rector whispered, and when they lifted a finger, a sun of Élan's ideas dawned above it. "First, Verve's current mission will advance our knowledge of the fifth transfiguration. Until then, I only have hypotheses about how Anima Reshapers work. Second..." Another finger raised, and a wormhole containing Élan's desires curled atop it. "—should you wish to evolve, you must first transfigure into a Protean to become the first true Full Transmuter besides myself."

"Who should I amalgamate? Which alchemist?" Élan demanded. They took a knee, folding their wings and looking up to beg for that clue to evolution. "Tell me their name, Rector, and I'll hunt them."

The Rector loomed over the other and pointed to the floor, where the mirror reflected a new silhouette. It mimicked Élan's position, but it blurred, shaped like them but not quite; not *yet*. Behind it, deep below the mirrors, lay the seed of another transfiguration.

Shocked, Élan fell to both knees, hands pressed beside the half-formed reflections.

"My Protean. My Anima! How? How!?" they stammered, choked by desire—but understanding eased them almost immediately. "Now that I know, a new transfiguration is possible!" They laughed, delighted, replenished with purpose. "Guide me and I shall follow, Rector," they murmured, and their voice split in two, a third whispering far away. "Who should I amalgamate? Who!?"

The Rector's scimitar grazed the floor, and Élan's new transfigurations moved. Between them appeared the clear, startling figure of a familiar Protean Reshaper.

"Vim..." Élan mumbled, recognising them, only to frown with another realisation. "Many single-transfiguration alchemists would treasure the opportunity of being more through others... but *not* Vim. And not others like them."

"Indeed," The Rector hummed, shrugging nonchalantly. "Not everyone would accept this change; some alchemists have not yet conquered their fear. Regardless, conflict is the cornerstone of evolution, and it will hasten the decay of our political order until the context forces us to define a new set of rules for the new reality."

"It could unleash an alchemical war..." Élan muttered, not daring to stand.

"It may, or it may not. It wouldn't be the first nor the last lodged on the records of The Orders." The Rector smirked, teasing. "Yes, Élan. Within our Library, somewhere and somewhen, such records exist. Now..." They leaned, pointing at Vim's reflection on the floor. "In five human years, I'll send Mien to Strezia; that tot needs a lesson on control and bias. That mission will also set the stage for you to amalgamate Vim; Hellion will assist you." They chuckled, vanishing and leaving only the echo of their voice. "Prepare Mien and yourself, Élan. I'll meet you again after Strezia."

Another bout of questions swarmed the Full Transmuter, melting them back into their shadow-formed body. For a long moment, they swirled over the reflections, until experience disabused them of the weight of such enquiries. The Rector's command had been clear. The path was laid out and it would happen as planned.

But even with that certainty, Élan knew nothing would stop them—not even the amalgamation of another alchemist. They would evolve. Their quest for self-improvement was their reason to exist.

"I'm the flavour of all knowledge and the compendium of understanding. I'm Élan," they repeated their Creed, like long ago half-Élan had done after their transfiguration.

Morphing back to their raven body, they flew through the Mirrors Room until it led them back to The Towers. Training was due.

Verve

5077 CE

The afternoon was doomed when Verve arrived at the greenhouse, alighting between Iúrdan's lectus and his working desks. Restraining their lightning, they glamoured the area from prying eyes and vanished their helmet; their ringlets of smoke fell loose, framing a four-eyed, flat countenance.

The stage was set, and their plan was simple. To force Iúrdan to reason and translate his intuitive knowledge—inaccessible to Verve—into a common language.

At that moment, the clinic's door shrieked open and closed, disguising Iúrdan's exhausted sigh and a few muttered curses. Verve soul-linked him at a distance, tracing the calm connection while his wet sandals spattered from the waiting room to the bedroom. The clothing racks creaked, tumbling as fabric slid from them, and the healer groaned again. Moments later, he dragged his wet bare feet across the corridors, approaching the glass doors. Calmness and peace spread through the soul-link as he pulled the latch, watching the greenery ahead, and finally entering the greenhouse.

In that dying dusk, there was peace. In the newborn night, there was chaos.

Fear poisoned the soul-link, pervasive and forceful, assaulting Iúrdan's thoughts as he took on the alchemist in front of him. His pale green eyes widened, his jaw fell agape, and strands of black hair framed his face, tickling his cheeks—but he stared, stunned as the glass door screeched closed, the latch popping back up. The noise startled him and all terror vanished as his logical peace returned, enforced and controlled, while purposefully ignoring his trotting heartbeat.

"An alchemist? I—ah..." Iúrdan stuttered, exhausted. He barely dipped his eyes, the bow minute and controlled. "I was not... expecting such honour."

"I did not announce myself either," Verve stated flatly, ignoring the strange greetings. They didn't threaten nor command, barely observing a truth as irrevocable as anything the human perceived.

Hesitating, he walked carefully, approaching the nearest table and glancing askance to take on the winged being twice his height.

"To what... do I owe this honour?" Iúrdan stuttered, unsure what to do with his hands—he clasped them in front, then behind, grazed the table's edge, and slipped them through his makeshift belt. "How can I... be of assistance?"

"Debate with me, Iúrdan. Answer my questions and I will leave after our conversation concludes," Verve proposed, polite to entice the human. "Our discussion will be neither correct nor incorrect. I will accept every idea regardless of what it is."

The healer scowled, lips pursed into a tight line; he was fighting a losing battle against the trembling of his jaw. A thousand questions flared through the soul-link, so clearly considered they emanated like strings of words. *What do they want to ask? Why me? Why here? Why not with those in the palace?*

His thought-voice chained him to a speechless position that uttered nothing else than an unintelligible stutter; it clogged the soul-link, stacking questions, echoing in his mind but never leaving his mouth. Verve waited, countenance impassive while they pretended not to hear anything.

A debate, it sounds... insane! But what if I refuse and—? No, impossible. The Orders don't attack humans without a reason... He glanced coyly to the wings, to the lightning, to the metal in their armour—and the soul-link calmed, wiped by the awareness of the uncontrollable. *It doesn't matter. I don't have a choice; If they want us to debate... that's it.* Iúrdan calmed, flooding the soul-link with a soothing thought-cadence. *This is out of my control. Just like with the illnesses, I can't control the alchemist. This is my present, nothing else. Struggle is natural; debating is all I can do.*

Verve awaited, amused by those thoughts. When they tilted their head, a sooty, smoke-made coil rolled over their engraved pauldrons. The gesture distracted the healer; he shuffled in place, licking his dry lips and ignoring the droplets trailing from his wet hair to pool on the floor. It took him a moment, but with his heart pounding in his ears, Iúrdan swallowed his questions.

"Ask, then... venerable one," he managed, voice restless and thin.

Delighted, the alchemist whispered the most obtuse question anyone could ask, "What is to be alive?"

"To struggle," Iúrdan answered without hesitation—and as he spoke, his fear vanished from the soul-link, replaced by the flat stance of a teacher stating the obvious. "Every journey through life is an arduous, dire path through failure and strife, sporadically blessed with an achievement, neither its frequency nor outcome proportional to one's efforts."

Verve's wings sparkled with lightning, their metal feathers chafing before they restrained it. Iúrdan's was correct. That link between identity and struggle was foundational to alchemy, and it brightened part of the soul-link—yet it wasn't enough. They needed to keep asking until Iúrdan translated every unexplainable thought into a shared language, reshaping his mental state enough for Verve to hypothesise on their true meaning.

A short-lived silence ensued, while two disparate gazes met.

"Indeed. Life is struggle, because to live is to skirmish against the fluid concept of identity," Verve countered, rolling a hand, the metal reflecting the incipient starlight that filtered into the greenhouse. "But what *is* identity?"

The healer blinked, shuffling in place. Closing his eyes, he breathed deeply, nodding to himself for a few moments—and the soul-link brightened with every breath, enticing the alchemist.

"Let us define identity as beliefs, traits, language, or appearance," Iúrdan lingered, strained with hesitation—but he cleared his throat, barely easing his frown. "Each of these... aspects has infinite variations; for example, we may speak the same language, but we reason through it differently. Therefore, although we can define the composition of identity, we cannot *limit* it. Identity is unique to an entity, and to the particular moment in which they exist..."

His voice thickened, gaining the cadence of a teacher, and that incipient confidence spread through the soul-link. Verve remained quiet, studying the connection—his alive elements within were morphing and reconstructing as Iúrdan voiced them.

"...from there, we may argue that everyone will struggle—to remain as they were, or to change. However, my profession taught me that... the struggle will take different shapes. It has diverse meanings, distinctive causes and consequences—as many as each person at any moment of their lives." Iúrdan smiled, meeting the alchemist's gaze, a teasing roguishness in his voice. "What everything alive has in common is the inherent resistance to the change enacted and enabled by that incessant struggle that defines identity."

A realisation dawned on the healer, and it blasted through the soul-link, dismantling the baffling elements. Their exterior crumbled, like mud dissolving to reveal the gemstone within, to fill the soul-link with memories.

Of Peiro adventuring and the forest defending itself. Of hunters and wolves, each struggling to kill the other and survive. Of flowers and herbs mulled for medicine, yet refusing to be crushed. Saustín, and the fire seeking air to grow and consume. The hail, shrieking as it bounced from the bloodied woman and shattered in the floor. Of the tree bursting with lightning, leaves cackling in a cry for life, branches falling to create new root. A thousand other cases, all presenting the same duality—people and a variety of half-alive elements.

The healer's voice was still echoing when Verve cocked their head, straining to analyse what the soul-link revealed. Iúrdan didn't posit the relationship between alive and half-alive elements; he neither deified nor anthropomorphised the latter, instead assuming that they acted due to emotions or instincts, behaving with an underlying *purpose*. Beneath that surface layer of ideas, the alchemist found another concept, subtle and barely translated into comprehensible worlds—those half-alive elements were somehow similar to *people*. Struggling, remembering, seeking, deciding.

Deeper yet, and before another heartbeat was spent, Verve unearthed another concept within Iúrdan's mind, confirmed by his prior choice of words—he had not assigned identity to people but to *everything alive*. It was a crude approximation, not to be taken literally nor compared to current alchemical concepts, but comprehended as did the human that had spoken it. The alchemist widened their eyes, scowling almost immediately; could Iúrdan be implying that half-alive elements behaved similarly to humans? That half-alive had an identity?

It was logical yet barely implied, an idea that Verve had not considered—yet they knew that this path of reasoning could lead to a concept far beyond a mere contradiction of alchemy. It could completely change alchemy and the relationship between alive and half-alive elements—and they had to corroborate it.

"Elaborate on the struggle. What struggles?" Verve hissed, demanding like a pupil whose comprehension depended on the confirmation of the sage teacher. "You said 'everything alive,' but thought of people and forces. You imagined the forest and hunters, and herbal medicine crafted for people. A blacksmith hurt by fire, a woman crushed by hail, people taking refuge from the lightning under a tree..." they lingered, slashing a hand in the air, demanding an answer. "Why? Why those thoughts?"

Iúrdan stepped back, thick brows furrowed. He scratched his cheek until the skin was as carmine as his cold, reddened nose.

"Because the elemental forces are not so different from people. They also struggle," he whispered, chin jutting to the potted plants, a hand waving to the flowerbeds. "A seed will struggle to blossom, even when sown on fertile soil. Fire will struggle not to be smothered by water or wind, and water will strife against boiling. The lightning is the extreme; its life is fleeting and powerful, but it struggles to exist and dies quietly because even its roar comes too late." He paused, scowling and rolling a finger. "Because these elemental forces struggle, they do so against people as well... they impose on us and we on them, adding to the uncontrollables that neither can, indeed, control."

Lightning rippled on the alchemist's wings, sparked by the thousand contradictions issued by such a statement.

"Nonsense. Struggle is a forceful fight for and against identity. Struggle exists because *identity* exists. *Someone* struggles because external wills affect their identity, and everything it implies," Verve retorted, a finger waving in denial. "Identity derives from consciousness."

The healer leaned forward as if sharing a secret. "Not always," he whispered, glancing down at the flowers. "Each fire, even the thunder or a plant, have individual identities. However, those identities are not comparable to humans'. They are different in nature."

"Except identity encompasses memories, experiences, relationships, and values that create one's sense of self," the alchemist rebuked, pointing down at the fire—it moved, as if avoiding them.

"But the fire remembers. Plants remember. Even the sound remembers... They have a self, because the self *is*," Iúrdan stated, gaping and struggling with the words. "It is just their memories and experiences are different in perception to a human's, and their relationship with the world is therefore dissimilar... which, again, leads to that interaction that reinforces the mutual struggle."

Iúrdan's idea was preposterous, irrational—half-alive elements had an identity. It was so sensible, so logical that Verve gave in—and the soul-link became comprehensible, intuitively so. Truthful, but not verifiable. Anything with an identity struggled. Half-alive elements had—

Verve lost all control. The world darkened; their body—the elements composing it—were out of their reach. They couldn't move or will it to change, just observe. Their elation over grazing the verge of new knowledge died as they caved into an overpowering mind-yoke.

One cast by The Rector.

A mind-yoke. It twisted ideas, it manipulated logic, it blended thoughts. It was an unwilling concession of control, a submission of one's existence to perceive and be as another so commanded. It was controlled by The Rector, their will so unyieldingly overwhelming that it coerced Verve's consciousness to watch, to think, to learn.

In that timeless moment, sailing between confusion and comprehension, they gained a new perception of the universe. Everything became bendable to one's will, coercible by one's thoughts, fleeting by one's standards of infinite existence. Everywhere and everywhen, anyhow and anyway, all elements coalesced in a way Verve could fathom but not.

This was an experience no other alchemist ever had the privilege of enjoying. The Rector's perception. The universe—no, existence itself—spread open like a blueprint of elements so structured and cohesive, and with a meaning so rational, there was no need to consider it. It existed as it existed; it evolved as it evolved. Factual, logical, intelligible.

Verve surrendered to it, uncaring of whatever this would mean to their own existence. Their own emotions surrounded them, dancing, twirling, fencing with each other. The exhilaration brought forth by the possibilities of learning gave way to the euphoria of toeing a line nobody else had, alongside the terror and ecstasy of reshaping themselves to become more. Always more.

'*Learn, Verve,*' The Rector mind-stated, four voices and a whisper. '*Learn like nobody else has.*'

Within the darkness, somewhere and somewhen, atemporal but temporal, Iúrdan was no longer. Only a cluster of alive elements, shapeless and indeterminate, formless yet alive, brimming with a clarity never perceived before. He was a compendium of memories, looming from a distant past, and altering his identity and knowledge through the stages in his life.

The Rector broke the mass of no-longer-Iúrdan, spreading it into a chart, logical and illogical, sound yet unsound. They discarded pieces, organising them, filing them with the methodical precision of a master at their craft. They flung pieces of identities, twisting emotions and sensations to catalogue thoughts, ideas, and beliefs. In that chaos, the darkness became a star field of alive elements, shimmering with flavours so far unknown—yet through The Rector, they became known to Verve.

Memories came first, part of Iúrdan's identity and essential to comprehending the world as he did.

A hundred patients flickered past, faces of all ages, of all shapes, of all places and times. Feelings surrounded them; care, concern, contentment, misery, merriment, sorrow, satisfaction, fury, forgiveness. Experience contained them, woven with threads of two facts—one, death was unavoidable; two, Iúrdan's skills were limited.

His had never been fearless apathy, never depending on the known. He had, on the contrary, lived thoroughly aware of the boundaries of his knowledge, and the race he was losing against death.

Peiro's bloodied face flashed, and the darkness burst with emotions and thoughts, chanting steps to heal like a chain to sanity. Iúrdan had sunk in a flurry of feelings and ideas, but never had they wondered about the *cause* of that wound. To the healer, to live was to struggle against the thousand juxtaposed wills that coexisted, sometimes contradicting each other, in the world. It could be someone's or something's, but it was, and it had an unstoppable effect, an irreversible consequence. According to that view, the wound was the focus; the present, never the past.

Dozens of other patients sprinted in the darkness, and Verve recognised each—they had been experiments, all of them; different, but all crafted to understand Iúrdan. The glittering shards—once mislabelled as embers of relief—had actually coated his thoughts, weaving a truth only now understood. Amidst existence, sentience would always struggle to explain struggle; to find its cause, to assign a reason, to analyse, to determine why, why one person, why in this way, why here, why now.

Those glittering, gleaming shards had never been relief, but *empathy*. One offered by Iúrdan to humans or half-alive elements, while embodying an affinity not even Proteans could achieve.

The forge burst then, consuming the darkness of knowledge. To Iúrdan, it had been just a fight to burn, not to be smothered or consumed. Nothing else than the struggle to live, just like the lightning slashing through the tree sought fuel, like the leaves contorted to survive, and the branches fell to take root again. Verve knew that everything was incorrect, but correct. Simultaneously, somehow.

Concepts came after, filtered and organised by The Rector.

Death and struggle were natural. The world's order, the rules of existence that everything with memory, experiences, or relationship endured. It had a spectrum, unknown but known, and it existed with flavours and scents, never the same, never comparable but always stretching over the sense of self.

Struggle was a *state*. A cause and consequence of identity, a cause and consequence of existence. Perceived, endured, and loathed.

In that darkness, within that mind-yoke, The Rector was a filter, translating the infinite concepts no-longer-Iúrdan had never clarified. They meld the alive elements, swirled them and coloured, rendered comprehensible to their immeasurable knowledge, and fed them to Verve through the mind-yoke.

One by one, piece by piece, Iúrdan's intuitions, contradictions, and world-changing ideas became part of Verve.

Someone moaned somewhere, anywhere. Blood bubbled somewhen, anywhen. A body stirred somehow, anyhow. In a greenhouse so distant, in a world so different. In an irrelevant clinic, a healer lay dying, mutilated but kept whole only as needed, body broken and mind mauled by the leader of The Orders.

Verve fixated on the moans, assessing them with the newly gained knowledge. The sound waves struggled, fighting to survive and expand their reach because neither required consciousness but implied existence. After the mind-yoke, that understanding was no longer contradictory. It was sensible and logic, even if disconnected from the rest of the alchemical rules.

That new knowledge, that truth unlocked, was an isolated boundary, separated by a gap from the bounds of known alchemy. It lacked a theorem to bridge it and explain its concepts. It was true. It was finally comprehensible.

For aeons, after wars barely remembered by The Rector, alchemists had believed half-alive elements to be *half*. Neither alive nor non-alive, they were limited by nature, answerable to will, and coercible after understanding its reactions. However, alive will could blend with half-alive elements—wind, fire, plants, thunder, and so many more—by tapping into the elements' struggle and identity.

That pair, struggle and identity, reshaped half-alive elements. Defined them. Combined them. Merged them.

Finally, Verve comprehended.

Sentience. Distant, unattainable. For now; *only* for now.

Sentience. Achievable within that new boundary.

Sentience. The goal behind the door opened by Iúrdan's ideas.

The marble was pure white, streaked with rivers of blood, mixed with flaked skin and handfuls of hair; nothing else than remnants, nothing else than decay. The greenhouse was glamoured, frozen in time and retracted from reality.

Verve fluttered their wings, metal and lightning sparkling alive, *struggling* to stabilise them. The world was suddenly dull, incomprehensible and enduring, too similar to Verve's own view, too dissimilar to The Rector's—and the Chimera-Warlord looked up, enthralled.

The Rector was there, hovering beneath the greenhouse's glass ceiling, existing in multiple dimensions and permeated by the plants on the tables. Twelve swords spread airborne like crowns of knowledge, six wings fluttering from their temples, arms of metal and wire forming a cloak, the pattern of existence swirling around them as if they enabled it.

Their image endured. Unfathomable and fleeting, yet seared on Verve's memory.

"You have too many questions, Verve..." The Rector stated, a hand pointing to the other, the scimitar hovering alongside it. "—but you also have a self, an ego... and it's damaged."

The Chimera-Warlord rustled their wings, soaring just enough for their boots not to mingle with the blood.

"I had to question him. I could not... *comprehend*, not even then..." They glanced at the remnants, at the space in-between, at the leader. "You *knew* this would happen, Rector, yet you sent me even while planning to arrive. Why?"

The Rector laughed, the twelve swords rattling. "Bias and boundaries," they whispered, the sound amused like the glimmer in their eyes. "Knowledge strengthens bias, stacking prejudices regarding the world's order, piling preferences to stain evidence, queuing opinions over preconceived ideas. Knowledge casts boundaries, and the more you comprehend, the stronger those limits become."

Verve's gaze wandered, dropping like a feather hovering in the wind, each arch linking ideas.

"Therefore, you are the most biased of all alchemists, the most bounded, the most limited." Verve lingered, carmine eyes narrowed to slits. "—which is why you did not send Hellion either. Their affinity for plants would have constrained them... perhaps even forbidding them from understanding."

"Indeed." The Rector bowed slightly in acknowledgement. "You, on the contrary, have always been too eager to reshape your identity through *learning*." They lingered, smiling like a proud teacher. "Many alchemists have the potential to trans-figure more than once, yet only a dozen had achieved it... and the answer is too simple. Acknowledging one's limitations is key to learn, and bias is the one constraint that will always lurk beneath someone's attitude—but you used the key I gave you and unlocked your new *self*. The—"

"The shroud was not caused by Iúrdan, nor by my lack of knowledge. It was simply a consequence of my bias," Verve interrupted, eager but factual, metal-feathers rustling. "After I noticed my prejudice, only the unexplainable remained; the knowledge beyond my boundaries."

"Which is another reason why I chose *you*," The Rector confessed, nonchalant. The swords repositioned to point at the other; when they spoke, their voice almost split. "If a single alchemist describes something, the observation and its description will be biased. Irrevocably so. If many alchemists, with different transfigurations, observe and describe... we may slowly produce the *unattainable*."

Verve chuckled, amused. "An objective truth..."

The Rector dipped their head, the blades folding back to resemble two wings. "Now, answer *my* question. What did you understand about Iúrdan's revolutionary idea?"

"It enables a fifth transfiguration with a new manipulation of existing elements," Verve groaned, soured. Lightning discharged inside their wings. "It hints at a combination of half-alive and alive elements, to create sentience... by somehow influencing the identity of a half-alive element. But—"

They gaped as their own understanding reshaped and recreated, supported by the new knowledge. It changed them, slowly yet brutally, not altering their appearance but the possibilities within—and The Rector grinned savagely while Verve clutched their chest.

"My elements, my composition... it *changed*. I felt it!" They stuttered, wings fluttering to regain balance. "Knowledge enables... evolution..." The alchemist paused, wide-eyed and looking down at the healer's remnants before urgency pushed them to soar as they demanded, "This is not enough! Iúrdan's is just a *truth* that we can't corroborate! He gave us only a hypothesis; we need the theorem. The hows and whys enabling this combination! We need more humans, more carriers of impossible ideas!"

The Rector laughed, and their joy cracked the world's order. "And we shall find them, Verve. In this age or another, we will find humans carrying this knowledge, thinking the unthinkable —and we will amalgamate them until their pieces bridge our gap of knowledge!"

"It's the only way..." Verve added, enthused and eager.

"Humans cannot develop their alchemical intuitions into systematic logic, but we do. Yet we are too biased to leap across our gap of knowledge," they spoke rapidly, encouraged by the leader's smile. "An amalgamation will incorporate their thought patterns into ours, to—"

"To unlock the secrets of the Anima Reshaper, and reforge ourselves!" The Rector cackled, and their twelve blades pointed at the bloody remnants, all wires coiling around. "This is the genesis of change, for The Orders and for existence itself!"

Dawn seeped through the edge of the world, the light spreading open upon colliding with the glass ceiling. The alchemists held their gazes, but a moment after, The Rector's body melted into the usual form Verve was accustomed to meet. They waved an arm, expanding the glamour to the entire clinic.

"In the meantime, return to The Towers and find Élan. Exchange what you learned with them… the raven one has a curious mission ahead of them," The Rector whispered, beckoning to the distance. "In five years, you will need to train them to master half-alive elements; after that, I will *finally* give you a new mentee… but not now. She is not ready yet." Mischievous, taunting, scheming. Both blades pointed southwards.

Verve chuckled, licking his lips, a finger raising as irreverent and rule-defying as they had always been. "I will teach both of them, but *you* will teach *me*. I need the new transfiguration, Rector. I need to evolve."

"Mull the knowledge I gave you, Verve… then visit the Mirrors Room. You already know what new possibilities await you there," The Rector whispered, the words sneaking on the bleeding edge of knowledge.

The scimitar moved, aligning between them to point at Verve's head before vanishing just like the four-transfigured alchemist. In that incipient dawn, the greenhouse was empty sans the multitudinous questions overpopulating Verve's mind. They melted back into their smoke-made body, rustling the trees and flowers, before their elation propelled them up—past the panels of the glass ceiling, and skywards into the free wind.

"I'm the euphoria of destruction and the zeal of reforging.

I'm Verve," they cackled, like long ago, someone who was not-Verve, had stated after their first transfiguration.

They would reforge themselves; it was unquestionable. It was their nature. Just like the silent truth that The Rector's mind-yoke had revealed.

The Orders would struggle; existence would struggle. Yet in the end, they would both evolve. Knowledge was infinite. Change was uncompromising. Progress was unrelenting.

Author's Notes

Thank you so much for reading *The Genesis of Change* and for your interest in the Author's Notes. It was a complicated novella to write and one that originated from two needs—to develop a magic system based on philosophy, and to discuss how knowledge biases a person... or, in this case, an alchemist.

Let me elaborate on the concept of bias...

Cognitive bias is a systematic error in thinking that happens when we interpret the information from our surroundings. It leads us to create a subjective reality exclusive to each person, and derived from our unique perception—which encompasses our knowledge, our training, our life experiences, our ideology and beliefs, and everything that makes us ourselves.

You could say that, to some extent, our identity biases us.

However, knowledge itself—namely, everything we know—is also a key factor surrounding our bias. The more we know, the more we try to fit our perceptions into the box delimited by it. But what specific type of knowledge does this? Everything! From the languages you know, the career you studied, the places where you lived, the customs you picked up, the skills you developed... every single thing has an added subjectivity once learned.

This is presented through Áurea and Verve.

Áurea struggles to learn alchemy because her human identity is limiting. Élan amalgamates other humans to give her multiple points of view to circumvent that bias... and once that's done, once she is frameless, she can transfigure. Basically, a key takeaway in Áurea's chapters (and disregarding the fantasy elements of alchemy) is that one way to reduce your bias is to try to understand other people's points of view.

Meanwhile, Verve struggles because they are at the "top of the chain" and they know *so much* that it is challenging to think outside of the box. Verve's bias has endured for 20,000 years (their life as an alchemist), and to add more problems, they *believe* to be objective! They perform experiments that corroborate their bias and, of course, end up "adding more logs to the fire" thus reinforcing their bias. Through the Chapters, we see how their disregard for humans and plants coat their actions, effectively steering them away from the evidence.

Now, let me add something. You are biased. I am biased. We are all biased.

The key problem with being prejudiced (as Verve states somewhere in Chapter 7) is that bias is unconscious, often contrary to our beliefs, and automatic. Therefore, we cannot just sit down and review it; we need to be confronted with situations that highlight the prejudice and then take actions to remediate it.

Overall, the biases types I leveraged for this novella are confirmation bias, the Dunning-Kruger effect, and selective perception.

THERE ARE OTHER THEMES...

Those additional themes are derived from the magic system. The alchemy for alive elements (the focus of this novella) is basically based on philosophy. *Mostly* (but not entirely or exhaustively), Stoicism.

The "atemporality" of emotions refers *mostly* to triggers. The interplay of fear and desire comes from a bunch of psychology things I read (I'm not a psychologist, mind you; my background is in software).

The idea of identity and struggle comes mostly from Stoicism. Lucius Seneca wrote, "No man is more unhappy than he who never faces adversity. For he is not permitted to prove himself", and also "Sometimes even to live is an act of courage." Marcus Aurelius' idea of "Our life is what our thoughts make it" inspired, alongside the dichotomy of control, Iúrdan's mindset.

Finally, I wrote and published *The Genesis of Change* in 2024, and am thoroughly aware that The Rector's pursuit of an alchemy to create sentience can be likened to generative artificial intelligence (AI), and the so-called "AI race". I did not write *The Genesis of Change* with that intent, but I acknowledge it can be read like that. Therefore, allow me to clarify that while I think AI can be useful if properly applied (e.g., enhanced security in cars, malware detection in email inboxes), I support human creators and do not use generative AI.

BUT WHY THESE THEMES?

Why did I write a novella about knowledge and bias? The short answer is *because I am biased*. The long answer is because I'm an ex-academic, and am thoroughly fed up with how academics subjectively peer-review research, deeming it useful or useless based only on their preference.

Depending the discipline, negative results may be considered utterly worthless, shameful, and never to be published (and yes, they could save others *so much time and effort*), and it is always deemed better (again, per discipline) a fancy and expensive method to get a minimal improvement, than an inexpensive and simple approach that performs well-enough (yes, I'm talking about Machine Learning research here).

There are far more cases of bias in academia than I could shoehorn into this little novella. *The Genesis of Change* may be part of my thematic response.

WHERE DO WE GO NOW?

The Genesis of Change is just a taste of what *The Records of the Orders* as a series will bring. Philosophy, eldritch alchemists with dubious morals, and plenty of hidden themes, mostly around knowledge.

If you want to read more, the next instalment is also a stand-alone and free-to-read. It is called *Mien* and follows Élan's apprentice in their mission to learn about control and bias.

Mien (the novel) is a book-with-choices, also known as text-based interactive fiction. It has two different endings, hides another knowledge-related theme, and even its structure is part of the overarching allegory. However, *Mien* is different to this novella, not only because of the interactivity but also because Mien (the main character) is a tot alchemist whose recently acquired and thus imperfect skills are incomparable to Verve's and Élan's. These two, besides being over 20,000 years old each, are among the top five alchemists of The Orders—the others being The Rector (it figures), Hellion, and someone not mentioned here.

If I convinced you to read *Mien*, you can access the book-with-choices through the app **Unearthed Stories**. This is a free mobile app available for Android (in Google Play) and iPhone/iPad (through AppStore); it is free to install, and the story is also free.

FINALLY...

My books are always theme-centred... and if these Author's Notes reveal anything else, it is how much I like to deep-dive and analyse books. My newsletter focus on that: exclusive insights into my series, including thematic details I share nowhere else. If that piqued your interest, you may sign up here:

That said, I honestly hope *The Genesis of Change* interested you. Thank you so much for reading.

Livia~

Acknowledgments

I am deeply thankful to every person who directly shaped this novella and helped me get it to where I envisioned it would be when I began dreaming about it.

To my partner in life and developmental editor, Fernando. Nothing would be the same without you; you are incredibly supportive, you give me hope, you give me courage. No language is enough to convey how grateful I am.

To my cat overlord, whose purring soothed me and who managed to immobilise my forearm and hand in a position where I could only write or pet him. I did both and regret nothing.

To my beta readers. You have been incredibly supportive and insightful in your critique. In particular to Angela (BookTuber at *Do Unicorns Read?*); your advise and your support was fundamental to get through this. Thank you.

To all my fellow authors and reviewers who read the ARC, provided reviews, and made the launch of this novella an incredibly exciting moment.

To Sarah Kempton, for giving voice to these characters and bearing with all my questions and details about the alchemists. I'm honoured to work with you.

Alchemical Glossary

Elements

Half-alive elements exist in nature and are tied to the cycles of a world. For example, fire, water, air, plants, spores, sound waves, lightning.

Non-alive elements do not have a progression tied to a world and do not exhibit behaviours. Examples are stones, metals, gas, wood (chopped), electricity (of multiple types, but not the sources).

Alive elements are mental states, thought patterns, and emotions derived from consciousness. It includes constructs such as identity, attitude, perception, and bias.

Transfigurations

Soul Transmuters. Known to humans as **Chimeras.** By knowledge and will, these alchemists can create, change, and destroy alive elements. They have a range of skills available, and the older the alchemist, the more skills they know, or the more information they can gather from them. Only specific alchemists, like Verve, can perceive alive elements without a skill.

Matter Transmuters. Known to humans as **Masons.** By

knowledge and will, they transform the statical chemical composition of non-alive elements. Alchemists of this type are often more proficient with one or two elements, but can create, alter, and manipulate all known non-alive elements.

Protean Reshapers. Known to humans as **Warlords**. Using their knowledge and will, they can create, alter, and manipulate half-alive elements. Like Masons, alchemists of this type are more proficient with one or two elements, something they refer to as *affinity*. Regardless, they can create, alter, and manipulate all known non-alive elements.

Machina Reshapers. Known to humans as **Devisers**. These are the only transfiguration that cannot be combined with any other—no alchemist, sans The Rector, ever transfigured into other class plus Machina Reshaper. They cannot create elements, but manipulate and combine non-alive with half-alive elements to create machinery and contraptions.

A double transfiguration is uncommon and challenging. Currently, there are only ten Full Transmuters (an alchemist who transfigured both Soul and Matter, like Élan). There are two Soul Transmuters with Protean Reshaper transfigurations—namely, Hellion and Verve. The only alchemist known to have performed the four transfigurations is The Rector; their real name is unknown to the other alchemists.

Soul Transmuter's Skills

Amalgamation. A fatal binding of a being's identity and mind to the will of a Soul Transmuter, lasting as long as the victim's self could endure.

Glamour. A skill shared across all transfigurations that allows the alchemist to create an illusion surrounding their body. They can glamour to invisibility, or create a human-like body that would move and seem to talk. Advanced alchemists can glamour entire areas.

Lore-weaving. A chimerical skill only available to Soul Transmuters. It is the inherent ability of reviewing an alchemist's own past knowledge without expenditure of time.

The more advanced the alchemist, the more detailed the memories, and the farther back in time the skill can stretch.

Mind-stretch. A Chimerical skill binding written words to an alchemist's will, to create a living, searchable index of content in their minds. This requires the alchemist to link to the physical writing.

Mind-yoke. A skill allowing a Soul Transmuter to experience whatever alchemy the controlling alchemist is performing. This is an unwilling concession of control, since the yoked one is an observer.

Soul-links. A skill that allows a Soul Transmuter to deep-dive into a single human's present emotions and thoughts. Advanced alchemists can go beyond conscious feelings and thoughts, to also perceive unconscious alive elements.

Soul-shape. A skill often considered a fable due to how unusual it is. It implies connecting to a single being, to perform a direct coercion of any type of alive-element. This can be as simple as a nudge (i.e., fostering emotions already present), or outright willing new emotions into the target.

Note that this summary of skills only encompasses those present in this story. There are more skills, especially within other transfigurations.